WICKED HALLOWS

THE SINS OF ALL HALLOWS EVE

Thank you

EMMALEIGH WYNTERS

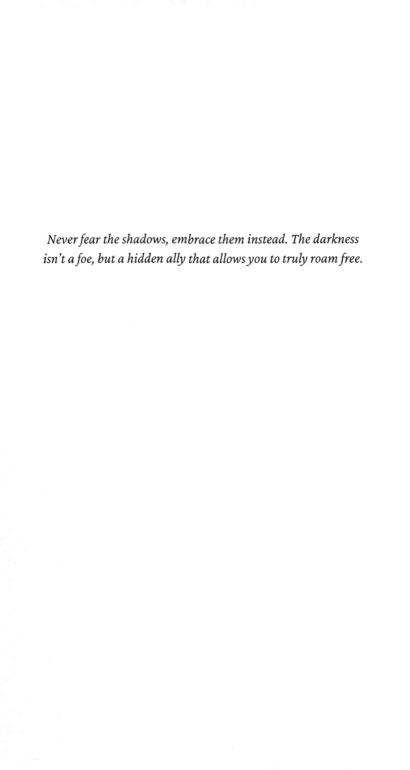

Never fear the shadows, embrace them instead. The darkness isn't a foe, but a hidden ally that allows you to truly roam free.

PROLOGUE

Welcome To The Circus - Five Finger Death Punch

The night was supposed to conceal our demons, keeping them hidden from the pure minds that would hang us for the morality that dwelt in their darkened hearts.

It was the one place where you would find your monsters lingering in the ominous shadows.

That was what we were told.

Every day of our lives, the things soaked in crimson were the things we should be wary of. That the ugly and the depraved were the sins we should burn with holy water, and every malicious thought should be purged from our minds and soul with an iron cross.

But when you play it right, the night was also the void that let our personal demons out to play with nobody to bear witness to such an incredible dark art of wickedness. Society couldn't condemn you for the sins cloaked in the veil of a lethal abyss.

We have been taught to think anything unholy was wrong.

But that was a lie and anybody still accustomed to such warped ways had my pity. We all held it within us.

A parasite that was waiting for the right time to consume your withering bones and installed you with the strength of a monster fit to rid this world of all its evils.

The night?

Had always been my favorite thing, no matter what side of it I got.

Just as the night covered my arms in darkness, so did the blood that ran in rivers down my wrists as crimson plasma splattered against my lips.

I stared back at the wall, seeing stars in the mayhem, and smirked to myself.

Why was blood so pretty?

Hmmm.

I ran my toes along the silken ground and smeared the essence that surrounded me as I went. Humming the theme song to *Stranger Things,* I licked my fingers clean before I kicked the body at my feet. Then, like a demon possessed, I threw myself onto the corpse and rained down maddening punches, licking the air that seemed to become electrified in my psychotic state. Everything tasted sweet and glorious, but I *needed* more. I let out a throaty sneer, putting *Scary Movie* and their what's uppp scene to shame as I lost myself to the rejuvenating euphoria that came with bloodshed at utter carnage.

Nobody talked about what a beautiful thing death was.

How final and complete.

Could a human brain even comprehend the magnitude of such a thing?

How we were here, until we weren't.

Until the lights went out and then we were where?

Nowhere and everywhere?

Well, I have a secret for you, sugar.

There was nothing after death. Nothing but torment from the thing that killed you.

Like so many others, that asshole's happily never ever would feature my twisted mug and my sexy as fuck sinister smirk.

As I carved the heart from her chest, I held it in my hand. Her pale face stunning under the light of the moon, breaking through the cracks. With eyes as dark as chocolate glossed over in a yellow sheen of crystalized balls, she stared back at me. It didn't feel like I thought it would. The heart was hard encased with squiggly edges—with curves and crevices that hide away all of the little valves that once kept this useless thing beating.

Now, I was eye to eye with it, holding it before my very face with a steady hand placed over my own heart. I just couldn't seem to feel the connection.

The horror.

The fear.

Which I presumed a normal person would. All I held was unbridled curiosity that coursed through my veins like burning embers of a great fire. I needed to know more. I needed to breach the barrier of inquisitiveness that kept me up at night. I needed to make some kind of sense of how I was alive, with a heart that beat under my palm and that was the only difference between me and the dead bitch beneath me.

Anyway.

Enough about me.

Welcome to the slaughterhouse, the place born of bloody desires and a curiosity that would most definitely kill the cat.

Happy Halloween!

CHAPTER
ONE

Ophelia
Monsters - Shinedown

D ark fog coiled around me as I kneeled into the cold, sodden soil which seeped through the fabric of my jeans. The rounded moon sat like a beacon of silver light that washed over me, highlighting parts of the grim and ominous graveyard in Hallows Point. Baleful clouds circled overhead, breaking apart the abyss, and forming sinister-looking images within the sky that had my pulse thundering under my skin. Throbbing with an acute awareness at the column of my throat with such force, it began to ache as if I had been stabbed with a needle.

I shouldn't be here.

I shouldn't be toying with the dead.

It was disrespectful, not to mention creepy as fuck.

The souls in these graves had either been blessed by the heavens or cursed by the devil himself. There was a feeling that burned into the back of my neck, deceptive eyes watched me from the shadows. It was in my head, I was alone here. I knew that. I knew that I shouldn't be here at all and the smart thing to do would be to pack up my shit and leave.

But I just couldn't help myself.

I wanted to know... *needed* to know.

How real such wicked words uttered on that one special night called All Hallows Eve could truly be. We all played into the feeble tales of such an unholy night.

Played the games of Bloody Mary and watched out for the Candyman with razor blades in his cut-throat sweets.

But what about the rest of it?

What about the demons of the dark?

My heart beat frantically, more wild than the stallions riding their way through autumn, churning those golden leaves. I could feel my pulse thumping against the taut skin at the column of my neck as I tried to build the courage to play with all things spooky.

This was a stupid idea, but there's no backing out now.

If I wanted my next book *Summoning Hell* in the *Shits & Giggles Of Purgatory* series to be another hit for me, I needed to do the research.

I needed to know what it felt like in the dead of night when you're alone, but never without company. When the darkness concealed your worst nightmares and you convinced yourself that something lingered there, in the shadows, waiting to destroy you with all the sick and twisted things you thought you had kept secret but were unable to in this very moment of a very bleak night.

The untamed pace of your horrified heart, that wanted any excuse to take you out of the game altogether instead of sitting idle and experiencing these acute feelings of terror.

Because being nothing was more than being a pathetic

human riddled with so much fear, it forced you to give in to those so-called irrational emotions that plagued the simplicity of a human mind.

I felt that way now, like I was moments away from succumbing to my self-induced terror and falling by the wayside onto some unknown person's grave.

I jotted everything down in my notebook.

Every little twitch and eye flicker and every little flutter and small seizure of fright.

Detailed every sensation and thought that was running havoc through my chaotic mind.

Everything from the chill skating down my spine to the tremble in my hands. The book beside me flickered in the wind as the pages flipped in a hurried arch, as if a galeforce wind had just blown upon it with harsh and unforgiving lips. I gasped, jumping back, bringing a quivering hand to my chest as the air around me burned like ice in my lungs, "For fuck's sake, pull it together, Ophelia." I slammed my hand down on the old leather bindings and huffed at the night. I found the book on some website that referred to themselves as the *Olden Truths Of Wiccan Ways*. I purchased the only thing they actually advertised on the site, actually. The description read that this was the only copy in existence and that only the one of pure blood could wield the spells within it.

Sounded like some shit marketing if you asked me, but I had to set the scene.

After I wandered through the graveyard aimlessly, I chose a spot at the back. It was barren, with dried, rotten and withered leaves laid along the ground. I wasn't disrespectful enough to do this over somebody's actual grave.

Sheesh.

A Weeping Willow tree that overhung, brushed against

the backs of my hands. The trunk was huge and spiraled into the earth beyond the canopy of weeping catkins.

The foliage seemed to glow a neon kind of deep and dark green, under the scarce light of the moon that reflected back at me as a dull kind of silver, now hidden from my vantage point at the moment. I rooted through my bag and pulled out the three blood-red candles, then set them down, embedded into the soil at the three tips of a triquetra. Then I sprinkled black salt around the iron pentagram buried under the dirt at the base of the tree.

"Jesus fuck. Feeling like you're about to have a damn aneurysm as the dead rise to eat your flesh definitely needs to be explained in the book," I uttered with a small whisper under my breath like the abyss would hear me and come for my soul if I uttered the words too loudly. "The things I do for my readers." My breath is harsh and chilled. A billowing white burst of cloudy smoke whispered from my lips as I shook my head and lowered my eyes back to the book, sitting by my knees.

I ran my deft fingers over the engraved cover. Gold foiled embroidery bordered the edge, curved and entwined like the symbols of a triquetra. The binding is one long and slithered snake twisted around another. Thick lips that looked to be coming out of the cover itself more than being added in some way, sat in the right hand bottom corner, and the title *Wicked Words Spoken On All Hallows* was scripted in such a deep and dark red above it, you could hardly read the words at all. I took a moment to appreciate the unique beauty of it before I flicked it open and found the page that I needed.

Anima Summoner

A spell that translated to Soul Summoner in Latin. The ingredients were the blood of the caster, a desire for the darkness, and the idea of the subject you wished to raise. In my case, a smut God from way down under. I pulled the knife out next and held open the pages with my knees, as I fought against the speed of the wind that funneled into small tornadoes around me and upheaved all of the dirt on the ground. My mind spiraled into what the fuck territory, but I had to see this through. I needed to experience absolutely everything if I was going to write it so accurately, my words would feel the way I was right now. My hair whipped around my face, the sharp strands barbed as I shook them away and pulled the blade across my palm. Blood dripped, small rivulets splotched against the soil, soaking them in the crimson tears of my very essence. I hissed, the pain not entirely unpleasant but unnatural as the sting spread through me like veins of fucked-up desire and heated my very core.

But we don't speak about that.

"Hear me, come to me, something wicked this way comes," I began to chant, the words raw and powerful as they tore from my throat. I felt it rushing through me, almost like the thought of this working alone was enough to empower me with a vicious tone that bespoke determination. It was enough to make a damn fool of myself inside a creepy graveyard too. "Hear me, come to me, something wicked this way comes." The tone of my voice increased in volume as it dropped to a deadly low octave, a low hum that sounded like the purr of an engine. "Hear me, come to me, something wicked this way comes." I glared up into the night as I willed all of my strength and focus into summoning this demon God. I risked a quick glance back down at the pages and read the next incantation like a damn pro.

Maybe I was a witch in my past life?

Huh.

"Come to me, wicked demon. A soul from the dark, a sinful heathen. I call to you, this Hallows Eve, to give you life and grant you a reprieve. Stain this earth red with my blood on your corpse, wreak your havoc as this night runs its course. I call to you now so let it be, rise from the ashes, and answer to me."

The sound of an explosion shattered my ears, but nothing seemed misplaced. Thrown back, I hit the ground hard and groaned as I rolled to my side and brought my knees up so I could lift myself back up onto them. "What the fuck was that?" I asked at the very same moment lightning struck and I shrieked like a siren getting whacked by the ship of sailors she was hoping to devour.

The sky flashed a neon-colored blue as the bolt of lightning that struck beside me shimmered in an angelic glitter-like purple. It was beautiful, you know if it wasn't trying to kill me dead.

Guess I was in the right place to keel over though, aye?

My chest burned as my throat turned dry, painful as I swallowed past the thick lump lodged within it. Sweat beaded along my brow, dropping onto my lashes as I batted them away and tried to settle my breathing that branded me like a hot iron. Thunder clapped across the heavens like a roar of demented deaths calling for the night and I shuddered, then folded within myself as I fell to my ass and lifted my knees to my chest in a cradle.

Unholy Satan, that was not supposed to happen.

What was supposed to happen?

Fuck if I knew.

But mother nature scaring the shit out of me at the exact moment I decided to do some in-the-field research for my next book was not one of them. I trembled as I spied something that looked like gray stone poking through the soil. I crawled toward it and swiped away all of the moist dirt and recoiled when I saw that it was a headstone.

A very neglected headstone.

Shit, fuck, Halloween cunt!

Here lies Blake Colton.

Not exactly poetic and heartfelt.

I did this on somebody's grave.

Damn.

"Oh shit," I breathed, as I stumbled back and forced myself up on unsteady legs. "Sorry dude, no disrespect!"

"None taken. But couldn't you have knocked first, given a guy the heads up? I mean, come now, love. I'm not even wearing my best face," a deep, brooding voice husked from the darkness as a man bled from the shadows and stepped through the overhang of the willow tree. I swallowed thickly, unsure if I should tuck my tail and run, or play dead to the man who stalked toward me with half a chiseled face of the exposed bones shaping his skeletal form. It weaved back together, regenerated, and connected to look like the side of his face thankfully covered in normal flesh.

Pain started in my neck as my spine locked up in terror. Everything within me seized in fright and disbelief, but the horror didn't stop the word from slipping out. "*Demon*," I breathed while the final piece of his flesh coiled and weaved back together and showcased an Adonis of a man before me.

He was striking, eyes darker than onyx with cheekbones as chiseled as Spike's from Buffy. Tanned flesh glistened under the rays of night, his entire body covered in tattoos. Not the kind that left no space on the skin, but the kind you ached to run your tongue over in the heart of one sinful and never spoken about again night. His chest and abdomen were on display as he wore a leather jacket that fell from his shoulders. My warped pussy fluttered as I clenched together my thighs.

He stood without shoes, toes twined within the soil, with black jeans hung low on his carved hips. The V that was sharper than any blade dipped between the waistline and stole my focus for a moment. There was something else that added to the sinister air around us though. Something that added to the feeling slithering all across my skin.

Blood.

He was covered in blood.

By the time I recovered from the sight before me, it was already too late.

He was there, in front of me with harsh breath that kissed against my skin and a vicious hand that coiled within my hair until he yanked me back far enough that he could expose my throat to him. Greedy eyes assessed me and everything fell silent. The only thing to be heard was the thunder of my hammering heart louder than the actual thunder that clapped around us.

His lips were a fraction away from mine as my hot air blew against them softly and he growled, "No demon, love. You did just bag yourself a serial killer though. Want to tell me how you brought me back from the dead? Because I'm pretty sure when my lights went out, they never came on again."

When his lips touched mine, nothing else mattered. The world fell away, broken piece by broken piece as it was taken by the breeze that took all of my sinful secrets to the void and I hoped they stayed far away from this sinful man.

CHAPTER
TWO

I felt my body as it trembled like I was running from a tidal wave that rose like the towers of Hell above me, ready to wipe me out with one brutal crash, "What. The. Fuck." I uttered with numb lips, unsure as to what the fuck just happened or why I stood slack in this man's unrelenting hold. It was brutal, domineering, and assertive and that alone had something wild stir in my core.

"You keep saying that, but it doesn't answer my question now does it?" He sneered as his grip tightened to the point of pain and a hiss of anguish escaped me. "How. The. Fuck. Am I alive and here, is the better question, don't you think?" He gritted out through clenched teeth and the cold and detached tone of his voice had my sick pussy fluttering at the sound.

"You really are a demon? It... It worked? Unholy Satan it worked!" I couldn't contain the odd excitement in my exclamation as I blew out a hard breath, right into his face and the force of it had him flickering his lashes in annoyance.

"Woman," he groused as he shook me. "Focus. I am not a damn demon. I'm a man. A man made of sinful, beautiful, depraved nightmares that will take your sugar cane fantasies and destroy them as I watch the life leave your yellow-tinged eyes. But I died. I can still feel it, coursing through me. Those last moments brought nothing but ice. A chill I couldn't seem to starve away," he trailed off, those last words came out like he was a million miles away, lost to the dark and harrowing clouds that seemed to be falling from the sky onto us like a shroud. "I can still feel it... So... Damn... Cold." He shuddered, eyes snapped to mine with intense focus and my soul jumped ship and ran. "I guess it's now your job to keep me warm, Soul Raiser." He smirked as he darted forward and gave me no option but to accept his lips pressed firmly against mine. My mind wanted to protest, but my traitorous body quivered with desire at his dominance. My lips cooled against his as I felt the coldness he referred to and understood exactly what he meant. That coldness could destroy me if I let it.

It didn't push me away though. I seemed to crave more of it instead.

It's clear I'd lost my fucking mind. Maybe some serial killer bled from the shadows and knocked my ass out with chloroform. An alive serial killer. If this is nothing but a hallucination though, would it be so deadly of me to play with this dark fantasy of mine?

The one we don't talk about.

The feeling of ice as it seeped into me was awakening, fulfilling, and somehow, despite my body temperature dropping, I'd never felt hotter. Like lava ran through my veins in boiling rivers of bubbled crimson. He worked his tongue into my mouth with a relentless passion, that had me mewling and placing my leg up to curve around his hip. He stared down at me with dark and unfeeling eyes, and mine snapped open in a warning. It was a mistake to look into those pools of death and violence, in that moment, he had stolen my soul and left me with the same hollowness that consumed him.

There was such a stark and dark confusion there I couldn't even begin to describe how fucking terrifying that look was, in the dead of night, hardly concealed at all by the shadows as the pupils widened, blown like a manic reacting to the first rays of light after being locked and bound in a dark and dingy dungeon for years.

With a growl and one hand, he lifted me. Hands cradled the rounded globes of my ass as he spun and backed us into the veil of the Willow Tree, the catkins brushed against my cheek as he placed my back straight up against the trunk. I purred, slender fingers weaving through the dark strands of his hair. I was lost in the throes of an unnatural passion that darkened my soul beyond the bleak abyss that I knew I kept hidden deep down inside of me.

He could use those dark secrets of mine against me.

I was unsure if I would fear or thrive on that little fact.

All that was left was a deep yearning hunger. I felt like I was on fire, my body was coming alive under his intensity. Then I noticed my arms curled around the back of his head. My skin was blue, the life rushing to the surface and being absorbed by his touch. I tried to pull away, to put distance between us but like a tongue to a winter pole, I was frozen.

As I redoubled my efforts, I managed to break free, "No! Enough!" I commanded as I writhed like a squirming cat trying to break free of an unwanted cuddle. My back scraped against the rough bark as the chipped wood splintered into my skin through the fabric of my shirt. He tried to move again, but it looked as if something was holding him back. Those chiseled features turned dark, darker than the evil air that swirled around us tempting us into sin. I managed to break free as I ran from him. He spun in a circle but made no move to follow me. It wasn't until I rounded a tree and flattened my back against it, hiding, that he popped up through the mist that had risen higher from the ground to conceal our shoulders and gave me a damn heart attack.

"What the fuck was that?" He asked, and I yelped and took off again, running in the other direction wondering what the fuck kind of Halloween fuckery is this shit.

"Why are you running from me?" He whispers over my shoulder, into my ear as I fell to the ground, tripping over a headstone. My heart thrashed against my ribs and I swear one of them cracked from the assault.

"Why are you following me?" I cried as I stumbled ungracefully back to legs that trembled. It was obvious, wasn't it? You run from the dead guys that chase you in graveyards, "Stop!" Was added in a shout that burst from me in vain. I fled the Skeleton man that felt the need to stalk me right now and hoped this was some kind of shadow-induced mind fuck.

I had *summoned,* the dead-ass serial killer that was now stalking me sounded more like it, my fucked-up brain parroted back to me.

As I glanced over my shoulder to see how much space had grown between us, I fall short when I don't see him anymore.

Like a lightbulb moment, it took a dark turn when I was cracked on the head with it.

Oh my god, this is the best possible outcome of my

research that I ever could have asked for. Too bad, I had to have a psychotic break to get the juice though.

How those diagnosed with a vault of insanity and have the opportunity to lose it altogether and experience this kind of shit and don't use it to become authors is beyond me.

Because I've fucking cracked.

As I turned back, my nose bumped against his and I fell on my ass again.

"Fuck, you have solid skin," I grunted, the bridge above my nose throbbing as he towers a good few feet over me. "You're corporeal?"

"Seems that way, love. It also seems like I'm attached to you. I've always wanted a pet, so this should be fun," he smirked as he leaned over to lift me from the ground with ease. "My naughty little, Soul Raiser. I'm going to have fun breaking you. I can taste it in the air, just how fucking sweet you'll be covered in blood for me."

CHAPTER
THREE

Ophelia

Bones - Imagine Dragons

"Would you stop that!" I berated as I watched this dude dance like a loon to the song that was playing through the speakers of my Jaguar. Turned out, that his method of killing, was to annoy somebody to fucking death. "If you think that I control you, why the hell didn't you stay behind like I told you to?" I questioned, my entire body stiff and riddled with tension as I death gripped the steering wheel.

"Because I'm attached to you, Soul Raiser. For whatever warped, catastrophic reason your little curious mind summoned me here, I think I'm here to stay. Can't say I'm too sorry about that fact. It's been a while since I could fist my dick." He teased as he moved his hand over the appendage that seemed to tent those black jeans of his.

"Don't you dare!" I burst out, cheeks scarlet as I side-eyed him.

He frowned, pouting like the devil who promised to deliver a world of sensual pain before slapping his pet on the ass with the incentive for bad behavior.

With a huff, he threw himself back into the seat, "Where's the fun in that?"

"I can't handle this. A demon. I asked for a sexy as fuck demon." I mumbled without sense, eyes trained on the murky road ahead but also on the odd and terrifying thing that sat beside me. Because no matter what, I knew he was not human. Not anymore. Not after I saw the skeleton that held structure to the skin.

I couldn't say that I wasn't curious, or that I never held a deep-rooted intrigue as to how the fuck all of this could have become possible.

Or that I wasn't attracted to this monstrous man.

But I could deny it until I was called on it, that's for sure.

How could anybody ever prove any different?

When lost inside a sea of insanity, ride the waves like a pro wearing a clown nose I'd guessed.

"Demon is subjective, pretty love. I'm sure many of my victims will tell you they definitely saw hell before I killed them."

The world around me stopped. "You really did that?" I asked lowly. "Kill people I mean?"

"Sure did, sugar. It was a riot. Now, are you going to tell me why you were playing with dark magic trying to summon a demon?"

I toyed with the idea of answering him. But if he had a taste for killing people, I sure as fuck never wanted to be on the receiving end of that wrath.

Fuck. That.

"I'm an author. I was doing research for a book I'm

writing," I uttered into the darkness of the car as I took a right turn down an uneven road.

"Big shot aye?" He chuckled darkly and I wanted to throat punch him so badly I death gripped the steering wheel until the leather squealed under my fist.

"Someday, asshole." I bit down on my tongue and drew blood the moment the insult slipped free. My eyes turned as wide as the ocean and swung to his as he deadpanned me stoically.

Shit. I'm going to die.

He was going to kill me dead.

Right here inside my pretty Jag.

Then he broke out laughing and my unease grew by the mile. "Asshole, huh? You got a sweet tongue there, Soul Raiser. I can't wait to taste it again," he mused as my heart sank and fell out of my damn ass into the seat that was moist from the sweat of my unease.

"Never. Going. To. Happen," I state as I fought for a smooth breath that never came. Suddenly, the road disappeared before me and I was left to stare up at the ceiling. My chair reclined and dropped out from under me as I plastered my back to it. A beat later, he was there, on top of me with my seat pushed back, my foot slammed onto the brake, and his knee firmly between my thighs with a hand collared around my throat.

"Never say never, babe. It's such a horrid word. You're mine now. My infatuation, my darkest desire, and my sweet little toy. Be a good girl, and I might just let you live instead of carving up this sinful little body of yours. It would be such a damn shame. You got that? Do as you're told and this will be a fun night, deny me and it will only be fun for one of us."

I tried to swallow.

I tried to talk.

I tried to think my way out of this, but it was as if my body craved a bloody and brutal death because I did none of the above. Instead, I lifted my own knee and dug it into his dick and smirked when he groaned, jaw tightened as his cheek twitched, then his tanned face turned a worrying shade of red. Something hot leaked from my core as my body shuddered at the power I felt at that moment. He tightened his hold and something raw and fucking savage had my smirk growing and tempting him to use more pressure. I kneed him again, rejoicing in the husked grunted groan that left him while he pumped his hips and pushed back against me for a harder and firmer feel as he rocked into the pain instead of shying away from it.

I arched my back and refused to tear my eyes away as they locked with his in a challenge. A challenge of who liked it to hurt more. I never claimed to be innocent, and if I was going to be stuck within the walls of my mind for a while, why not enjoy it while I could? I decided there and then that I'd give myself to the delicious and devious lure of tonight. If I woke up tomorrow and it had all been a dream it sure as fuck would have been an inspiring one. If this is real...?

Well I could lie to myself for a while longer could I not?

He sniffed me, leaning down a little lower, a little closer. The air was intimate in a sinister kind of way. "Hmm, there is something wicked in you, pretty girl. I can smell it."

I hiked a brow, a smile pulling at my lips. I felt a little evil, tired of forever playing nice. Tonight was a special kind of night though, one where monsters were unbound, uncaged, and free to roam this tainted earth in all their glory.

Tonight, I wanted to be one of those monsters, fucked

up and freed from the sheep's clothing of a bitch as I walked into Halloween as a sexy version of Michael Myers.

"You want to play, baby girl? Let's fucking play."

"And how, oh dark one, do you want to play?" I whispered, my lips a teased against his.

"The only way you can play, love. With a whole lot of blood and a hell of a lot of screams."

CHAPTER
FOUR

Blake
Daredevil - Stellar

O*h, how good it felt to be undead, back from the dead under a pretty little witch's spell.*

With a shiny new toy to boot.

Perfect throat.

Perfect body with curves in all the right places.

Tits as ample as a dead man could dream.

Fuck yeah, this was going to be a good damn night.

She was as stunning as she was warped.

I saw it there, lingering within those green beryl's.

The curiosity. The need to know.

There was something wicked in my little soul raiser. And I fucking thrived from it.

How the fuck she even brought me back from the dead, I didn't know and I didn't want to know.

My mama raised me to never look a gift horse in the mouth.

Just used to pull out their tongue and had a party with it.

Horses and raves.

A real good time.

Let your freak flag fly and all that.

That was my motto.

"You want me to kill somebody with you?" she asked and I smirked down at her like the beast that I was. I wanted so much more than that, I wanted it all. All of that darkness, all of that immorality, I knew she held too much too tightly. I wanted all of her sins and then some.

"I want you to watch me kill somebody and then scream my fucking name when I fuck you within an inch of your life on some dead fuckers corpse who will never have the pleasure of feeling how fucking tight you feel clamped around them," I told her, making sure my voice bespoke sinister tales and depraved desires that this long night would bear witness to. That I would *pull* her into.

I saw her pleading with me within those dark eyes of hers, the eyes that are begging me to take away the choice. To allow her to experience what it's like living on the other side of what is deemed right and wrong, without having to accept the consequence it took on one's soul.

I'd never been a man to deny such a sweet thing.

Why would I start now?

So, I'd oblige and I'd show her exactly how liberating taking a life felt.

I leaned down, kissing her harshly before a dark chuckle escaped me and I regretfully worked my way from on top of her and lounged back in my seat. She bolted upright, a look of horror in her wide eyes as she glared back at me. "You're fucking crazy. That's-that is sick! It's—"

I cut her off with a shrug. "—It's life. We all live and we all die. Old age is just a myth, sweetheart. Whether it's a disease that gets ya or the hands of a bad boy devil, we all die in the end."

Wasn't that a fact?

I never pretended to be a kind man, in fact, I was far fucking from it. And evil is subjective to the snotty-nosed bitch judging it. "Pull out your phone," I ordered and she looked back at me with those faux doe-eyes in confusion. "Now, Soul Raiser. The night is waiting."

"Why the fuck would I need my phone?" she asked with an attitude I could not wait to spank out of her.

"Blake Colton. Google it."

She stared at me again and I tapped my knuckles against the dash in annoyance. "I'm as much a patient man as I am a nice man, love. Don't keep me waiting."

With a huff, her fingers flew over the screen and the irritating click of the keys made me grit my jaw in agitation. Her tense posture deflated as I watched her scroll. She relaxed back and slumped in her seat as she flipped through article after article. I smirked, knowing what she would be reading *and* loving that I could take her perception and twist it to make my skewed and corrupt life make some kind of twisted sense.

"You killed the bad guys," she whispered in a low mutter, almost to herself. "So... you're a good guy?"

I recoiled like she just threw holy water over me. "The fuck I am, woman. I might kill the worst evil, but don't even think for a second I'm not exactly that... Evil."

Slowly and controlled, her eyes came up to meet mine as we shared a moment that had my skin pebbled in a way I was not familiar with. I shuddered, shook it off, and nodded my head in her direction as I turned to gaze out of the window. "Pick one."

"Pick one of what?"

"Pick a victim," I stated and a moment of silence fell between us. I knew she wanted to argue, that she refused to move with the intention that this would all go away and she could go back to the life of a lie, but I would never give her that option. "It's not like you have a choice, and if I have to keep repeating myself, we are going to have a problem, sugar." I opened the car door and stepped out, ready to round the car and take the driver's seat when the tires squealed and the vehicle shot down the road. Something from the center of my chest tore free, a sinners soul that pulled taut like a rubber band and incorporeal like the breaks in a cloud of smoke. Before I could growl, I was back in the car, her body trapped in between my thighs once again as I was thrown back into the steering wheel at the same time my head thumped back against the ceiling.

She shrieked and threw on the brakes.

Fuck, I might be dead but the pain was as real as if I was still alive. The ache in my back spread, filtering through my shoulder blades and I had to crank my neck and grit my teeth to keep from throttling her.

What a shame it would be.

But I won't kill her.

Not until I had seen the blood that would soon stain her hands.

My dick hardened, thickening at the thought as it ground against her when I flexed back and tried to shake away the tenderness of my spine.

"Fuck," I groused. "What part of attached do you not understand, woman?"

"The attached part, now get the fuck off of me," she

snapped back, and it made me all the more excited to corrupt this pretty little thing beneath me.

"Oh yeah, this night is going to be real damn good. Now. Pick. A. Fucking. Victim, woman, or I promise you'll be my first kill of the night."

CHAPTER
FIVE

Ophelia
Super Villain - Stiletto & Silent Child

How could I choose a life to end? What gave me the right to play judge and jury?

But I couldn't deny that there was a deep-rooted longing inside of me that wanted to play the executioner. To rid the world of one more evil. One more sick and perverted person who stained this earth.

I looked back at Blake and knew there would be no way out of this. No way to escape the man that was attached to me and if I wanted to live to see Halloween, I'd need to play ball. What officer could save me from a dead man? And honestly, did I really want to be saved? There was something cold inside of me, deep beneath the sea of humanity and I couldn't lie and say that I had never thought about it.

Ending a life.

Seeing the lights go out in a repulsive man's beady little eyes.

I blinked then looked down at the phone on the passenger seat.

I didn't even need to pick it up in order to know where I wanted to go.

Who I wanted to kill.

He gripped my jaw, his vise brutal as he fought back his temper at my endless attempt to rid myself of him.

I huffed in resignation and nodded my head. "Fine. I have someone," I whispered, so quietly I hoped the world would swallow it whole and never use those words against me for the rest of my days.

"Good girl. A real good, good girl," he praised with approval in his dark pools that swirled like the lure of an onyx abyss. He tightened his hold until my mouth popped open and he placed his thumb inside. I clamped down around him by instinct. His chilling touch warmed around my hot mouth and I quivered, sucking deeply until my mouth had swallowed his thumb whole. The sensuality of such a strange moment had something hot in my chest.

I had no idea what my traitorous body was playing at while I was tempting the devil. Why I felt euphoric at the promise of ecstasy.

He was a drug, one I wanted to chase down the rabbit hole if only to get a bitter taste of the hatter and his fanatical view of the world.

I moaned, my tongue swirling up, down and around his thumb as his other hand fisted my dark hair, using his power as a guide to move me at his will. "Soon, this will be more than my thumb and when it is, you will swallow it all. Am I clear, darling?"

I nodded, helpless and at his mercy. I needed a reprieve, I needed the ache between my thighs to subside just so I could think straight again and remember that all of this was *wrong*.

So very fucking wrong.

"Now, get out. I'm driving," he ordered, and I listened. Like a lamb to the slaughter, I walked around to the passenger side of the Jag and cemented my fate when I closed the door behind me.

"Hmm, being my good little blood whore looks great on you, love. Now, tell me who we're killing on this fine night of All Hallows' Eve?" He raised a brow and watched me expectantly as I told him the street. He seemed to know it, meaning he was from around here which is not at all surprising considering the articles told me as much.

He was murdered when he was twenty-seven. Taken hostage by a rogue cop. Tortured to death, skin peeled from his flesh. The cop was more demented than the man who sat beside me, I knew that for certain. The only thing just about the cop's method of punishment was the injustice of it all. He only did what he did because Blake took out his partner.

A sex trafficker.

Good fucking riddance, if you asked me.

The world wasn't black and white. Sometimes, I envied those brave enough to step into the gray.

I shook my head, wanting to get rid of the parts of me that could understand this. That could accept what was about to happen tonight.

We took a left and pulled onto the street of my choosing, a massive church sat sprawled before us. Towering into the sky like it was in pursuit of the heavens, but even those who worshiped here were not quite pure enough to touch it.

Figures.

"A priest, huh? Good girl gone bad... I like it." I rolled my eyes and swallowed thickly, my unease growing as the nerves in my core coiled into one hot mess that had me fearing bringing up yesterday's dinner in revulsion.

"Come on then, love, death waits for now, scaredy cat."

As I got out of the car, I curled in on myself hoping I could blend with the shadows, in hopes he may forget that I was even here at all. No such luck. A heavy hand fell on my nape and I was directed to the front doors of the church and hesitated, only to have him push me forward until I stumbled through them and fell to my knees.

"Such a good look on you. Maybe you should just stay down there while I show you how it's done, yes, babe?" The arrogance on the Adonis before me was stifling and I narrowed my eyes to mere slits of fury as I stood back up on my feet.

"Fuck you," I hissed.

"Fire. Such fire. Hmmm, can you smell it?" He chuckled deeply, darkly and it sent chills feathering down my spine.

"You're fucking crazy."

"Duh, come now. Let's go catch a body."

I followed him down the aisle slowly, keeping a few feet between us. Like a mouse, creeping on a cat in the wild, I took every step tentatively. When we rounded the front pew, he looked around in search of the priest and I struck like a hound from Hell as I jumped on his back and shoved his head in the bowl of holy water.

I meant... it was not actually a bowl, but I also was not a religious person so fuck knows what it was actually called. All I knew was that it was supposed to send this fucker right back to purgatory.

"Go back to Hell, motherfucker, and come back as a sexy-ass demon like I asked for in the first place," I hissed like a demented feline having a bitch fit. Wishing for a demon was still probably very idiotic considering I couldn't even handle a guy that was once human.

But hey.

I wished that I could.

He struggled under my weight, the slosh of water rimmed over the bowl and splattered at our feet. The sound of broken breaths and lungs filled with water echoed around me and I cringed because that sound... it was the sound of death and that was exactly why he brought me here.

With a roar, he threw me from his back and I fell to the ground with a wheeze. He turned slowly, methodically and the shadows seemed to rush to his aid in a cloak of malice so daunting that it took me a moment to replace the fear in my heart with the will to survive his anger. Although it wasn't anger that glared back at me, it was twisted amusement as he heaved a deep, clean breath, coughing up the water stowed in the back of his throat.

Rivulets of it beaded along his brows and one stray drop tethered on the edge of the tip of his defined nose. His dark hair curled and glistened from the rays of light to the liquid that dampened it. I swallowed thickly as I tried to hide the lust soaring in my veins. The need burning in my core. My nails dug into the long holy rug thing that lined the walkway in an attempt to stay stoic. To not have to show this man the war in my core.

"I'm most definitely your demon, Soul Raiser. But I'll let you in on a little fun fact. You can't kill your demons when they know how to swim." The smirk on his lips was a battle on everything impure inside of me fighting for everything sinister that plagued me like a disease.

The devil on my shoulder was winning and she was

winning on her back with her legs spread wide in invitation more than ready for his sweet, depraved invasion.

Fuck.

He launched himself at me, both hands clamped down on my hips in a bruising hold as his fingerprints marred my flesh. He lifted me from the ground like I weighed nothing, high in the air and above his head with some whacked inhuman strength. I kicked and I screamed, batting at his arms before he set me down on my feet, fisted my hair at the crown of my head, and shoved my face into the torrent of water that swirled around me like a tsunami. It burned, it burned so fucking bad as I breathed in the water that wasn't made to be inhaled like it was laughing gas. I thrashed and I writhed as I fought for purchase. My eyes were wide open and burning as I saw my own reflection at the end of the endless chasms that were trying to kill me.

Consume, and devour me in its watery grave.

I panicked. I soared and I even felt a little euphoric.

This close to death, this close to feeling so fucking alive even as my struggle dwindled and my lungs filled with the end of my life as I knew it, I still couldn't help but feel free.

It was a mind fuck.

A twisted sense of a well of emotions I could not even begin to navigate.

I didn't want to die. But I didn't want to lose this feeling either.

"What's going on here?" A withered voice asked, and I could hardly hear it through the blockage in my ears.

But clear as day, I heard Blake's reply, "Oh you know, just trying to kill our sins. Want to try it?"

Then I fell to the ground, panting for every breath as Blake stalked the priest like a vicious reaper risen for All Hallows' Eve.

CHAPTER
SIX

Blake
Devil Inside - CRMNL

I t was a beautiful thing.

First the confusion and then the fear.

It became so potent, that you could smell it in the air.

Don't listen when someone told you emotions are scentless because it was bullshit.

That sweetness? The thing that wafted to your nose and made you all jittery?

It was dread.

And you were the cause.

"Sorry about that, man. My girl wanted to play. Now, here's what's happening because I know that's the question you're chanting inside that sick and perverted head of yours." I tapped my temple and gave him my winning smile as I stalked toward him with the grin of a loon on my lopsided lips as he tripped over his own feet. "We're going to play trick or treat. You trick me, you die. You treat me, well... I'll give you the sweetest treat of all. Your life." I stood before him, the tips of my bare toes touching his ankle as he laid flat on his back staring up at me with horror-filled eyes, mute as the flames of Hell that threatened to consume him and drag him right down under.

Oh, this was the best part. I could feel it in my ice-cold veins. This one, he would be as wicked as they came. I could see it in the hollowness of his eyes. How his unkempt hair tumbled down to touch with his lashes in flops of shaggy curls in an effort so that he could appear hipper. More approachable to the innocent kids he took under his wing. In the crow lines around his eyes that were formed from one too many days overindulging in what made him the most happiest.

But I won't say it though.

I won't tell you the sick and immoral things this pervert has done.

I won't put his sins out there into the world.

I couldn't.

Because if I did, I'd become unhinged. So unhinged it would become a compulsion to kill. I'd be a man possessed and I would miss half the fun in murdering this piece of fucking shit dead and showing my girl what she was missing playing the prim and proper beauty who never got blood under her nails.

Who the fuck could live like that?

"So, let's begin, shall we?"

"I-I, I don't—" he sobbed, those tears one-hundred and ten percent authentic. Here was why cunts like this were the most genuine when their judgment card was called. They walked through the life they took for granted all willy-nilly, eradicating innocent lives with their perversions. It was a gift of mine to see through those perversions. A perk of being a dead man.

Because you could never lie to the dead.

Men like this?

They took and they never gave back.

They destroyed but they never, *ever* fixed.

But why, oh why, did they cry the hardest?

It was because they became so drugged up on their twisted vice, they really never gave death a second thought and when it came knocking, the sight of it was enough to make them plead like a fucking slob, but never enough to clean their hands free of their sins.

They feared what they thought would never touch them.

People like me, however, welcomed death.

Men like me?

We *lived* with death.

We danced with it under the mistress of the moon and welcomed it when our time came with open fucking arms.

Fuckers like this?

Well to put it simply, they felt like the world owed them something.

News flash. This world owes you nothing.

You wanted it?

You fucking earned it.

Earn it, then fucking take it.

Just like I was about to earn this man's life with the prize of staining my hands in his pretty crimson. Another soul to add to the tally of the ones that I'd stolen.

I looked over my shoulder and winked at Ophelia. "Pay attention, love. I'm about to show you a work of art." Then I looked back at the mess of a cunt weeping at my feet.

Disgusting. I could feel the patheticness from here. "What are your sins, priest? Do they out deprave my own?"

"I-I'm innocent! A man of the cloth! A man of God!" he screamed, eyes bloodshot as I tilted my head with cold, dead eyes. I gave him a chance to fix that trick before it cost him more than a wicked lie spoken.

When he didn't, I fucking smiled.

"Trick it is then." I turned and helped my soul raiser to her feet and brought her to my side. "You're going to want to see this, sugar."

Her gasp was the loudest thing in the church when I cracked my neck and convulsed in static energy that had my appearance flashing between the handsome man that I was and the dead, curdled, decayed demise of my skeletal form that lay rotting beneath the skin.

The shift from this plane to the next allowed me to find the lies that screamed for justice within the small particles of the air, unseen by the naked eye. It was just a thing I could do. Now I was alive, I could sense there was a lot of things I could do.

We all had them, sins that shouted to be held accountable for the darkest things they did in the dead of night. Humans just never seen them floating around their heads, begging for attention, begging for acquittal. That was where men like me came in.

"Demon! The child of Satan! Oh lord, save me! Save me from this unholy man!" As he clutched the cross that fell around his neck and down his chest, I rolled my eyes in displeasure.

I may need to rethink this demon thing.

If Ophelia wanted me to be her nightmare, I would show her the dark side as soon as I was done here. I'd be her demon and when she ran for the hills screaming because she bit off more than she could chew, I'd keep her anyway.

"Winner, winner, sinful liar told tales to a fucked up killer," I singsonged before I glanced at my girl again. "Just call me a dead-man lie detector, babe. Thing is, this is a bad, bad man. He does bad bad things. Question is, can you read between the lines?" I waited for her to get my meaning, to understand my words and when the priest tried to crab-crawl backward, I kicked him lazily in the chest as I heard him thump back to the ground never having taken my eyes from hers.

Ophelia's eyes widened when it finally dawned on her. "He didn't!" she hissed in outrage as she looked down at him in disgust, a new awareness in her fierce gaze. He averted his eyes, unable to meet hers in fear she would see the truth he wished to keep hidden within them.

"Oh, but he did, love. Fifteen minutes ago to be precise. Look at his pants." I never needed to, I'd already seen the cum stain all over the fly. "So, pretty lady. Would you have me set this man free?"

A test.

A choice.

The hand of the devil.

Would she take it?

I knew she would...

Now, she would become who I knew she craved to be, no matter how much she denied it, I had woken a dark creature inside of her that thrived for all things bad.

After a moment of silence, an internal war on morals, she squared her shoulders and brought her cold complexities to hold mine. "Kill him." Then she turned, took a seat, and crossed one leg over the other as she prepared to watch.

Got to admit, she caved a lot quicker than I thought she would but in all honesty, decent human beings didn't play when it came to this shit.

We protected kids.

When the truth that there were monsters that went bump in the night, but they are one hundred percent human and not some *Monsters, Inc.* bullshit, it hit us differently.

It became all too real and the need to protect the next child became much greater than the need to protect our souls.

"That's my girl," I uttered under my breath. "Looks like All Hallows' brought you a ticket out of here. Tell the devil I said hey on your way down." Then, I took my time. Nice and slow so he could feel the pressure building before I killed him with the oppression of the intense anticipation.

Thick golden ropes hung from the obnoxious beams that arched overhead, threaded down onto a runner which allowed them to string up massive embroidered and obtuse crosses either side of where he stood every Sunday, like a god to his people. I pulled on the lever, the offensive crosses crashed to the ground. Tying his ankles with the rope, I pulled the lever once again and hung him before us by his ankles and smirked as the blood immediately drained from his face, turning it even more ashen than it was moments before.

He bellowed and he screamed, hoping somebody passing by on this frightful night would come to his aid. The fucker was shit out of luck because all he had was us.

And I didn't know the meaning of the word mercy and soon, neither would she.

"What are you going to do?" she asked in an almost sultry whisper and my dick hardened.

The scene, the sounds, and by Satan her fucking scent, it was enough to have my cock heavy and raw, gripped by a brutal ache. I could feel it pulsating, all the blood in my appendage demanding all of her attention. Every last inch of it. I was a desperate man, a desperate man that needed a reprieve from the violent lust that tore me to shreds in a soul burning, deep arousal.

Soon.

I'd fix that soon.

Now, I wanted to hear her answer.

"Slit his throat," she commanded without hesitation this time. Like a regal queen sat on her throne. Any compassion she had for him before she knew his truth was long fucking gone. She shut down, turned it off, and focused that hate into an energy that was singled-minded.

She wanted blood.

Her fucks to give were buried under a layer of ice that continued still, hardening her heart.

"Hmm," I moaned, adjusting myself. Then I had a better idea and I unzipped my pants. My gaze found hers in a silent demand. She rose to her feet and prowled closer, right before me where she fell to her knees with pools of lust so thick in her complexities, that they darkened the green, turning them black.

Those pretty eyes were ones of unburdened desire.

My favorite fucking shade.

And fuck me if it didn't look great on her.

Slender fingers curled around me and I shuddered, the coldness to her touch a welcomed acquittal. A funny kind of acquittal when my cock is guilty as fuck from wanting to use her in any way that I pleased.

I patted my back pocket and found my knife. Figured if I appeared the way I looked when I died, all hippy-rock and barefoot looking and shit minus the flayed flesh which must be the reason why I could go all skeletal and shit, then I should have some of the cool toys I died with still on me. "Jackpot," I growled, as the priest swung back and forth trying to free himself and gain a reprieve from the head rush. He thrashed as wild as a shark strung up on a dock craving to breathe in the salt water once more.

"Oh God, no! Please, God, no no no. Don't do this. Don't kill me. I don't want to die!" he chanted, lost to his terror, and fucking hell, it was a beautiful thing.

It electrified my fucking frozen solid, cold as ice, blood.

"God won't save you, asshole. You just have me and the devil tonight," I uttered, my gaze focused solely on Ophelia. Her eyes fell half ladened in lust, heavy and baked as she lost herself to this sensual moment between us. Her chest heaved, and every tender breath had her ample tits rising from the effort. Thick lips parted softly, sweet sounds whispering past them and her head fell back on her shoulders.

"Open your mouth, gorgeous," I encouraged, as the head of my cock slipped across the seam of her lips as smooth as silk. I glared at the swinging pinata and heaved a deep breath trying to center myself from the feel of her so close to where I needed her most. When she tilted her head back and opened to me with the offering a man would kill for, without an ounce of uncertainty I drew back and slit the priest's throat. As soon as the first rays of his silken blood splashed outward in a stunning arch like an umbrella that sprayed her thick and fuckable lips red, I jutted my hips forward and thrusted deep into the back of her throat. Her shoulders rose as she breathed me in, pulling my dick taut as she inhaled and sucked me mercilessly as I fucked the sweet tasting crimson deeper into the back of her mouth with beautiful savagery. "Oh, fuck me. That's it, Soul Raiser, bring my dick back to life."

The intensity in her gaze fucking burned, everything was so fucking hot. Too hot for a man that was so fucking cold.

The heat of her warm mouth, the air around us. The cries of a monster and the ominous feeling that filled me with euphoria.

It was all too stifling.

All too compressive.

And I couldn't wait to combust under its flames.

I siphoned the body heat from her, enough to take her to that place of bliss I knew she felt in the graveyard, but not enough to kill her. Just enough to take us both to the place of nothingness that we craved. The place where everything fell quiet and you finally knew peace.

I rocked and swirled, fucking her mouth in every rhythm possible. She licked and teased the under shaft of my engorged cock, doing unthinkable things with her mouth considering I never pulled out enough for her to even kiss the head of my angry beast.

Brutal, raw, relentless. I showed her not an ounce of mercy as I used her, as I sadistically and ferally made her feel every fucking part of me. Every thick and hardened inch slid with ease to the back of her throat as if I belonged.

I *knew* I belonged.

Tears welled in her dark emeralds, as I fisted my hand through the silken strands of her chestnut-brown hair, and curled the ends around my lower wrist so I could tug, *hard*. She fell slack, giving me everything I demanded. I smirked, stroking her cheek with a tender thumb as I wiped away the tears that fell before bringing them to my lips.

"Hmm, you taste so fucking good, baby. So fucking perfect when you cry for me."

Long lashes fluttered. I reached out, tapping the end of her chin in command to look at what I had done. To watch the man die as he bled all over us like a sacrifice to the universe that made rising on All Hallows' Eve possible.

We were covered and stood under his rain of crimson as he spluttered and choked. The sound was one of the most harrowing sounds a living person could ever hear.

It was the sound of a person dying in such anguish, that you could feel it in your soul, or lack of a soul even. It reached you even in the darkness, in the void of an abyss that became you and made you feel something, even if you felt nothing.

He was alive, but already dead and he knew it. It showed in the white yellowing of his eyes as like a sand clock, his time ran toward its end.

And I was forcing him to feel every second of it.

Having your throat slit was no easy thing. It was messy, it was brutal and it made you feel every inch of the fucking pain before it stole away the last living thing inside of you.

Hope.

It was long and it was one of the most barbaric tortures you could inflict on a person. It was a pleasure that we got to witness every fucking second of it.

The shock, the confusion, the moment it all went numb only for the pain to reawaken you with a stark slash to your senses that you gasped, forgetting you had no air left at all to save you. The moment that the tanned face of a human dwindles into an ashen man drained and then into the yellow-stained corpse that waited for the devil to claim his rotten soul.

I lost control, this game I was playing with her boiled to

a point of no return. I fucked her tight mouth with abandon. I had never been a saint, one foot always in the grave, and fuck me, the place I came from had no good folks corner. I walked at the devil's side, tearing apart the monsters in the night and now I was here, fucking the tunnel to heaven and I couldn't hold it back anymore.

With a roar, I let my devil out and sank deep, holding the back of her head and lodging myself into the back of her throat so tightly, that I knew the air was a struggle. So, I pinched her nose, becoming the hand of her fate and the devil she would worship as I decided whether she would live or die in this moment of ecstasy.

I stared into her eyes, showing her my darkness. There was nothing gentle in my gaze. Just a question and with the look she held in hers, I knew I had all my answers.

I was having way too much fun to kill her now anyway, especially considering how fucking pretty my girl looked on her knees.

I didn't know how this night would end.

If I would stay undead, or if I would return to Hell.

Either way, I might not have killed her at this moment in time, but if the night decided to take me home again, I knew I'd be taking her with me.

As I shot my load and felt her swallow everything I had to offer, milking me dry, I pulled out and traced the seam of her lips with my thumb. "That's my good girl," I praised as she smiled back at me with a coy smirk but also with the lust of a siren in her dark, dark eyes.

Fucking beautiful.

CHAPTER
SEVEN

Ophelia

Bad - Royal Deluxe

I was weak. I tasted the seed of the devil and now I needed more. Beyond research, beyond human curiosity, I was aflame in a dark desire that licked against my sensitive flesh in a way that felt so bad, that I was quickly forgetting what it felt like to be good.

By human standards, I should have felt something other than high at having enabled a murder. Something other than excitement and warped inquisitiveness that had my interest peaked and my heart racing.

A fucking *murder*.

But *pheww,* I was free of the burden of even having felt a drop of sorrow or regret.

Fuck me, it was impossible. I never needed Blake to spell it out. This bloke was fucking scum. A cliché if I had ever seen one.

But that was the thing about it, right?

We expected people like this to be far and wide. Never

in our reach. Not on our very own doorstep. I brought Blake here to drown his ass in holy water and free myself of the monster I had accidentally summoned, not kill a pedophile.

But here we were.

Right before me, strung up like a Halloween treat.

As he promised, he showed me the other side of human impulse. He filled the curiosity of what would happen if we tested all those dark thoughts we have in the quiet and never told anybody about.

Because it would be wrong, wouldn't it?

To take a life?

Why though?

Because some asshole sat behind a desk decided to divide humanity and gave special privileges to those in power and with a badge, then expected us little people, the people who were already powerless, already the prey, to play the victim instead of taking our pound of flesh?

I stood and bounced on the balls of my feet. There was a new kind of energy that was coursing through my veins and it wasn't just the buzz of having a man like Blake hold all of the power. My lungs burned as he cut off my airways, but I had never felt more in control. More empowered knowing that I was the reason he got to finish. Everything about me was a desire he couldn't resist.

I was afraid, lost to what should be and not what I wanted to be.

A dark angel, a vigilante, and a savior for the weak that thrived in the shadows of the dark. I wanted to be more than an author writing about the pretty depth of profound words. I wanted to be an author who fucking lived them.

"You seem excited, darling. See something you like?" Blake questioned and the dark tone of his voice snapped me back into reality. I was living inside of my mind. In a fantasy of one night being the purge and allowing us to let it all out.

But this wasn't the purge.

It was Halloween and as the night went on, it got creepier and fucking creepier.

Right now, I'd be more scared of myself than anything else.

I never knew I was capable of such hate.

That I was capable of telling him to kill a man.

And yet here we stood.

I never even questioned it. When the dark thoughts of innocent cries and blood-stained souls that were broken by a man who took a vow with God to always protect them surfaced, something inside of me snapped. I say the first words, the first feeling of hate that consumed my soul, and beyond that, I let everything else fall away. I felt nothing beyond the need to watch this sick man cry for us. Beg for the mercy that he never gave any of those children. I couldn't. There was no room for mercy when my soul was full of such hate.

"It's okay, Soul Raiser. It's okay to want to hurt those who do bad things. After all, the devil might be real, but God isn't. If not for us, who the fuck would get justice for those who have been hurt? Because it sure as shit would not be the government, and it sure as fuck wouldn't be some figment of good that has never shown this world an ounce of grace." He stalked toward me and lifted my chin with the tip of his index finger. I gazed up and stared into his dark and soul-reaching complexities, my breathing slowed as he stared back at me, and all I saw there was the truth, the truth of this dark and hateful world. "They like to paint us black, love. Make us the monsters that walk this earth… The cold and immoral creatures who do wrong and depraved things, but the truth is, we're the ones saving it."

I was struck mute because I had never thought of it that way before.

It was a truth we had been conditioned to overlook, to second guess when it crept into the dark recesses of our minds and we then convinced ourselves there was something wrong with us. Any time we had this violent urge to right our wrongs.

The *truth* was we were all capable of murder, it was just who we murdered that mattered.

I inhaled deeply, then turned my face into his hold, nuzzled open his hand, and rested my face in his cool palm. "I don't know who the fuck you are, Blake, or where you came from, but I know that I need you to keep this feeling alive," I whispered.

When you only had a night to be unbound, would you waste it?

Judge me or join me, but we all died in the end anyway.

I refused to meet my maker with regrets.

"Then we have more work to do, love. Because I don't know how long you'll have it." He feathered against my lips as he teased me. I wasn't naive enough to know this wasn't a mind fuck, a way for him to seep inside of me and take hold with brutal claws.

If I was a sensible woman, I'd fight it.

But right now, I was a drowning woman and I wanted him to keep me under.

"I know how this ends, Blake. But I won't be your victim," I warned him and he smirked against me. My eyes fluttered close, sinking into the feeling of him that surrounded me in utter bliss.

"Smart girl," he mused. "Naughty girl. I believe punishment is in order for trying to drown me though, don't you?" The sensual mood changed in a second when he lifted me. My legs instinctively wrapped around his waist as I gasped.

He carried me toward a confessional and kicked open the door, caging us within the small space as he kicked it shut again behind us. With inhuman strength, he lifted me high over his head as he pinned me to the surprisingly sturdy wooden wall. I had to crane my neck, the wall not offering any height beyond one person. How I was placed, with my core to his mouth, I was kissing the ceiling and when he breathed cool breath against my hot core, I couldn't say that I'd complained.

"For each sin, you confess, I'll grant you one orgasm. For each lie, I'll make you beg for Hell," he whispered as I tried to focus on those words over the pulsating within my ears, the blood rushing to my head. My heart beat frantically, painfully, as my ribs ached in protest. I was flustered, hot and heavy, and needed something to give.

I had an itch, one I needed help to scratch.

"Blake," I breathed, never having felt like this before. It was like he was inside of me, awakening me and touching every deep-rooted part of me that had been hidden for all of these years. He lit me up with euphoria. He was an ancient kind of power that seeped beneath the surface and sunk vicious claws into my spine, keeping me rooted to nothing but him.

"Confess, Ophelia," he demanded, his tone harsh and so fucking hot as his hold on the tops of my thighs tightened. I could feel the outline of his fingers branding themselves into my flesh and I flexed, hoping they'd leave a beautiful mark.

I shook my head, rolling it side to side at a loss of what I could say. I was uncertain whether I wanted to run from this overwhelming sensation or give myself over to it, on my knees with an open soul. I was hot and bothered, my mind a thick haze and he hadn't even touched me yet. I was still wearing my jeans, and the cool air of his breath seeped through the fabric. Something sharp dug into my hip, my eyes snapped open as his growl reverberated through me and he dragged his hand down my thighs as I sat neatly on his shoulders. The seam of my jeans dissolved and they fell from me with ease and draped over his arms that held me. Then "Follow Me Down" By The Pretty Reckless started to whisper around us and I shuddered as if the voice was a sensual feather that caressed my oversensitive flesh.

"You have powers?" I gasped, freaky skull thing aside, he seemed so human. Just as I thought it, he shifted again and it was the half-skeletal man that stood before me.

"I have the ability to take what I want, after all, I am a dead man. We have to have some perks," he mused lowly as his gaze transfixed on my core that wept for his attention, almost as if it was absent in his mind and the only room he had for thought, was on what fluttered before him.

I quivered, flexing my hips to get closer to his mouth.

The thing my body burned for the most.

He pulled back and turned those non-negotiable eyes to mine. "Confess."

"What the fuck do you want me to confess?" I hissed as I twitched in arousal.

"A sin."

"Fine!" I blurted then said the first thing that came to my mind. "Freaky hot serial killers turn me the fuck on!"

He chuckled against me and I bucked at the unexpected sensation. A cool tongue swiped across my core and dampened my panties before sinful teeth ripped them aside.

Then he feasted on me like I was his last meal, the air he needed to breathe.

A lifeline.

A shot of the best fucking whisky that saw you through to the end of a very glorious night.

"One orgasm for one confession," he mumbled into my cunt and the vibrations twisted me into something feral. I couldn't rock or find a rhythm. I was seized and convulsing under an unnatural tongue that drew inhuman sensations from me like a tidal wave that shattered against the shore.

I came harder than I'd ever come in my life. The stars fell from the sky and danced in my vision. Darkness encroached, and I faded for a moment before a stark uproar electrified my blood and had me bolting back upright to attention.

"Another," he demanded.

I shook my head in refusal. "No, I can't," I panted.

"Another sin, Ophelia." Fuck, the way he said my name was a sin.

This whole fucking night was a sin.

He pinched my clit and I spasmed, squirming away from his touch. "Okay, okay!" I shouted as I tried to think. "I liked it," I breathed into the silence that fell.

He left it lingering there with what felt like a tender beckoning from his mind, before he asked, "Liked what, love?"

He already knew. I knew he did.

But the fucker would make me say it anyway.

"I liked watching you kill a man. I liked knowing I was a part of that bastard never walking the earth again. I liked how you used me, how you pleased me. I liked it all, okay!" I blew out a harsh breath and for a moment, nothing happened at all. Then I found myself adding more to my confession than I planned. "It felt like I had just jumped from a cliff only to dive into the chilly waters and not crash like a comic book character falling from the sky. I felt like I had been stabbed with a spike of adrenaline that lit my entire body up from the inside out. I'd never felt anything like it before. Like I was an addict and this was the high they craved. I felt numb, raw, and utterly lifted beyond depravity. I- I felt happy. I felt free."

Once the tension drained from my body and the weight of that burden lifted, I stared down at him only to see him smirking back up at me.

Then he made me come all over again. Squirting into his mouth as he sucked on my clit like a man possessed and the pressure there had me blacking out.

Dead man's tongue, I didn't think I could survive another orgasm even if I tried.

CHAPTER EIGHT

Ophelia
Kill the Lights - Set It Off

I had nothing left. My mind was blank as I felt myself being carried. Soft sinful whispers of praise filtered around me as my head lolled against a hard shoulder. Something cool and wet trailed against my core and I would have shuddered if I wasn't lingering in limbo. Material coiled back around my thighs and I never even had the energy to open my eyes and see what was happening.

As I wavered in and out of a blissful state, I managed to blink open my eyes only to see the stars pass me by like shots of silver liquid. A low hum vibrated through me and a burly hand wrapped around the top of my thigh. By the time I heard something closing behind me and felt the sensation of being carried again, I was more lucid.

"W-where are we?" I mumbled into his chest, then began to wonder if I had actually taken something because an orgasm that made a girl dwell in a void of pleasure for this long surely wasn't natural.

Well, the dude is dead so I guessed that wasn't natural either.

As he carried me up the steps, awareness came rushing back to me. "My house? How the fuck did you know where I lived?" I almost shrieked, the idea of getting away from him now and having a safe haven to hide was long gone.

But truthfully, I'm not sure I wanted to hide anymore. I never killed the priest. There should be no evidence that linked me to the crime and the scum was just that, fucking scum who deserved to die. When Blake returned to the grave—which I was sure he had to do at some point or we would be entering the land of zombie zone and zombie dick which would be just *wrong*—then all of his crimes must go along with him. Why shouldn't I dive deeper into my research? Why shouldn't I see what it meant and what it took to be a killer? Slowly saving the youth of our church one fucked-up priest at a time?

Was it really that wrong when we thought about it?

Morals aside.

Nobody could argue with fucking morals.

Fuck.

My head was spinning. I didn't know what the fuck I was supposed to feel or think anymore. I was lost to a warped kind of confusion that had the power to infuse me with strength as much as it had the power to kill me under the weight of the infliction.

I was at war with myself.

The only escape I had was to give over control. After all, I was being held hostage by a dead man.

A dead *serial killer.*

Would it not be easier to put the blame onto him?

Deluding myself into this being a game of survival and not a game of suppressed desires and curiosity.

You'd be lying if you said you'd never thought about what it would feel like to take a life or to watch one being taken while you stood idly by and took it all in.

Let's not blur the lines.

Bad men deserved to die.

Sometimes, it really was that simple.

I heaved a breath and looked up at him as he stared forward stoically, not a fracture in that burly and chiseled face of his. "Driver's license," he mumbled before he cracked a lopsided smirk and my ovaries squirmed.

"Right," I uttered.

"I cleaned you back up at the church, then drove us home. You were kind of out of it," he explained as he got to my front door. I shimmied in his arms in an effort to look for my keys but he held me tighter. So tight, I could hardly breathe as I was melded to his body like we were one, then like it was nothing, he walked through the fucking door and my heart stopped.

I waited for the impact. For my body to bounce off the frame and send my ass tumbling back down the steps. None of which happened. Instead, a coldness crept through me. I felt weightless as if the breeze had caressed my cheek and I had become one with the wind and on the other side, I did what any sane person would do.

I shrieked like a bobcat.

"What the fuck was that!" I hissed, then shivered uncontrollably. "You just walked through a fucking door. With me in your goddamn arms!"

"Okay, Captain Obvious." He chuckled with a stupid, arrogant look on his sexy as the dead fucking face.

I was far from amused. "I'm not dead, asshole! I'm not made to walk through doors. I feel—I feel... Violated!" I mumbled as I clawed my way free from his arms. He put me down with a dark laugh and I scowled at him.

"After all the things I did to you, Soul Raiser, walking through a door made you feel dirty?"

"Ergh!" I huffed with exertion as I threw my hands into the air. "This is wrong, so very very wrong!"

"Or so beautifully, very fucking right," he countered with ease like this was just some ordinary day for him.

"You get brought back from the dead a lot?" I questioned with a hike of a brow suddenly thinking I should have asked this oh-so-obvious question before.

"Can't say that I do," he singsonged and my ire only grew.

"Why are we here anyway?"

"You need to rest and I need to pick our next victim," he told me while he moseyed about my living room looking at everything with a keen eye and I trembled, a sensitive chill skating down my spine as he assessed where I was.

He ruffled through the papers on my desk and I hurried over to him, knocking them out of his hand with narrowed eyes. "You are messy," he stated. "If that doesn't speak big time author, I don't know what does." Then he sent the last piece in his hand floating back down on top of the others." Go rest, I'll find our next kill."

"Next? We are not doing this again." I chuckled like a crazy person. My sanity fraying as I scoffed in mentally strained amusement.

"Oh, love. We definitely are."

"*Not.*"

"Can you go and argue with yourself in your sleep? It will save us time for when we get to our next location. Because we totally *are* continuing on."

"Sure, fine. Whatever. I mean, it's not like you can make

me." I smirked as I stalked toward my bedroom. Before I went to dream of the impossible, I stopped and turned back toward him as he was now searching the photos dotted about with a hint of sorrowed envy in his gaze. "Is the Devil really real?"

"Yes," he answered without looking at me.

"But God isn't?"

"Nope."

"How?"

"Humans, babe," he sighed in what seemed like soul-deep tiredness and it was so potent, it had me physically stifling a yawn. "It's in your nature to justify the bad things with something good. They created this being, this thing, to throw their blind faith into not knowing that, in itself, was the true monster. Your very own capability to lie to yourselves."

I blinked at him, not too sure how to answer that because deniability was a human's most toxic trait.

He had made a lot of sense tonight and I was not sure if I vibed with it.

Hopefully, by the time I slept off the numb legs and quivering limbs, he would be gone.

No such fucking luck.

CHAPTER
NINE

Blake
What He Don't Know - Anarbor

S illy, sinfully beautiful, shit out of luck woman of mine.

She thought this would stop.

That *I* would stop.

I'm only just getting started in showing her what it was like to be without your inhibitions.

To be free of the ever-growing burdens of humanity.

The utter lack of fucks to give about what society thought.

Her place was definitely a home for the creative. There were notes about ideas for stories and character arcs all over the place. Whatever the fuck a *character arc* was, I didn't know. I fingered the corner of a note on a doe-eyed woman summoning an alpha-hole demon on All Hallows' Eve and had to hold my stomach as I laughed.

Well, she may not have gotten her demon but she most certainly got her monster.

I threw myself onto the couch and kicked my feet up on the coffee table, upheaving more crap that she had left on there. I placed my head back, staring up at the ceiling. I couldn't say being brought back from the dead was a normal occurrence, but it was definitely an interesting one. It was fun corrupting my Soul Raiser. Watching the innocence war with her depravity. It was a form of fucking art, honestly, I'd have that dodgy cop flay me a million times over if we ended back up here.

She was my new little toy and I was having way too much fun to give it all up now.

I hadn't felt this alive since my last kill, the one where I took out my murderer's crooked partner. He was next on my list, but hey, ho.

He got to me before I got to him.

That wouldn't happen twice.

I grin cruelly just thinking about it.

About all the sick and vile things I would do to him.

All of the sick and vile things that fucking cunt did to *me*.

I couldn't say anger was an emotion I had much of. I was more familiar with *'it is what it is'* type of emotion.

I was that kind of guy.

And what it was for me, what it'd always *been* for me was... excitement.

Jubilation. Passion.

A job I fucking loved doing.

Making the world a better place, one twisted fuck at a time.

After I rested, my thoughts spiraled and my excitement grew.

I wanted this to be as good for Ophelia as it would be

for me. So I got my ass up and stalked back toward her desk and grabbed her laptop.

Fuck sitting there though, even the office seat had clutter. I headed back to the couch, threw myself onto it, and kicked my feet back up on the coffee table before I opened the laptop. Naturally, it was password protected, but dead guys don't need to worry about that shit. I placed my finger over the scanner and overrode the electrical crap and then I was in. Opening the web browser, I puckered my lips as the anticipation grew.

Oh, this was going to be good, I could feel it.

Local Arrests.

The search engine brought up pages of results from my request and I idly scrolled through them as I tried to pinpoint the best victim. The list of charges were endless. Theft is petty but didn't warrant the urges I needed to purge.

Rape. Hmm, I guessed I could butcher a penis or two. I mean, if you couldn't handle the gift of a cock, then you didn't really deserve one in my humble opinion.

I mean, life without a good fuck?

Kill me twice.

I was looking for something a little more interesting though.

Something a little more creative than the standard shit.

There were all kinds of fucked up people in this world, I wanted to show Ophelia the worst of them. After all, the worse the crime, the more euphoric the punishment for the ones who had the privilege to dish it out.

Bingo.

That case would be perfect.

I tucked that little nugget away for later and kept scrolling.

Oh *shit*, I chuckled as I turned my head to gaze out of the huge bay windows in Ophelia's living room. Out into the quiet street where unsuspecting neighbors slept through the witching hour without a clue as to what severe turpitude surrounded them.

I mean, I knew bad guys were a stone's throw away, but even I was surprised that this case is so local.

This dude was a killer alright. A killer with a fetish for eating his victims.

The news report even quoted him as saying he couldn't eat one of his victim's pussy because it was too chewy.

I mean...

Now I was insulted.

Another prick who didn't appreciate the fine, fine aspects of a human body.

He was definitely next on my hit list. But first, I had to get my head in the game and get rid of this irritation for the fuckers who got away with murder.

And by got away with it, I meant got to live with air still in their lungs behind bars for the rest of their lives.

As I closed the laptop, I placed it beside me and stood to my feet, stalking through the living room and out into the hall. The house was quirky, cluttered, but homey. Nothing worth noting. Once you had seen one home, you had seen them all. Although this one belonged to my woman, so I found myself gazing around as I hunted her.

The walls were a light gray, but most of the place was a darker, sleet-gray brick. It was a house built on cozy, grounded aesthetics and I kind of dug that.

As I reached the doors, I pushed them open with the toe of my bare feet and peered inside, stopping once I found her bedroom.

She lay there, sprawled across the bed in absolutely

nothing. In a heap of limbs tangled within the sheets, she looked as if she had just gotten home from a night on the town and stripped herself naked, unaware of her surroundings.

Alpha pride burned in my chest knowing I showed her that good of a time in the confessional. I quivered, a low growl slipped free as the taste of her began to taunt my senses once again.

I wasn't complaining.

She was right where I needed her.

By the light of the moon to guide me through the darkness of the shadows.

I prowled toward the foot of the bed and stopped, just gazing down at her and appreciating every fine and delicate curve of her creamy flesh. Two dimples sat low in her back, the rounded globes of her ass sat plump and protruded and I itched to squeeze them. Slow and methodically, I lowered, like a king in the jungle that artfully stalked its prey, I crawled toward her. My hand was imprinted into the mattress but I remained silent. I dropped my head, placed it between her thighs, then inhaled deeply. Drawing her sweetness into the dead lungs that thrived for such a treat. I groaned lowly, a shudder skated through me as I fought back the urge to pounce. Slowly, I palmed the cheeks of her ass and moved my face upward, smashing my face in between her cheeks and dispelling the breath I had held within my burning chest. The small gush of air tickled her and she mewled, eyes closed as she remained in a peaceful slumber. I blew once more, allowing her to feel the sensations in her soul before I jutted out my tongue and licked her beckoning star.

Once, twice, three times until she purred.

Then I moved lower once more as I circled her opening

in a tease her sleep-ridden brain couldn't quite work out before I speared her with it. Licking, sucking, and penetrating her from behind.

Fuck me, she tasted so fucking good.

Sweeter than sin.

The definition in fact.

She was everything and I was a withering man under the wickedness of her glory.

I growled and the sound vibrated through me and into her, a shared connection that had her squirming. I pulled away slowly, wanting to play with her more than I had ever wanted to play with anyone.

I wanted to torture her as much as I pleased her.

I wanted her tears and I wanted her praise.

I wanted her body coated in a sheen of sweat, reeking of our entwined scents.

I wanted it all.

Her pain and her satisfaction.

For a chick that was out summoning the dead, she must have a few candles laying around here. I rummaged through her drawers, moving from dresser to dresser until I hit the jackpot.

Yes.

It was perfect.

I had a lighter in my leather jacket, so I was good to get this party started. I pulled it from the inner pocket and walked back toward the bed. Her ass was stuck out more now, her knees almost to her chest as she hugged her pillow and sighed softly.

She'd hate me for this when she woke up.

She'd love me for it too.

I leaned over, plastered my front to her back, and whispered in her ear, "Wakey wakey, Soul Raiser. The night is still young."

She groaned and burrowed closer to the pillow, sticking her ass into my groin and grinding against me. I snarled in restraint and she whispered sleepily, "I thought you'd be gone."

"Not likely, love. The man of death himself would have to come and take me from you."

"You are dead," she deadpanned.

"Yet, here I am... With you," I answered. "Do you trust me? Trust me to make you feel good?" The husk in my tone was a caress to the side of her face.

"That's about all I trust you with," She replied and I knew she was awake enough, giving me consent to do this with her.

To her.

"Good, now hold still because this will be a shock to that sleepy mind of yours, sugar." The smug sound in my voice made me preen even more with pride. I massaged the cheeks of her ass before I parted them. Then I sucked my fingers and made sure her ass was nice and wet. Although something told me my woman would love the feel of the burn that was about to come next.

Slowly, experimentally, I placed the end of the candle stick into her ass and she gasped, her body reacted trying to shoot forward, but I held her steady with my weight.

"What the fuck?" she cried, then panted and a small moan of enjoyment slipped out.

"Trust me," I rasped, thick and heavy with lust. "Just trust me."

I could feel it as her toes curled and her legs strained. As her breathing grew sensual and she relaxed back into the bed. I saw it as her back arched and her slender fingers fisted the sheets and her head rolled to the side, her eyes closed in pleasure as she ground against the bed.

Fuck, my woman is dirty.

"Can you feel that, baby?"

"Hmm-mm," she hummed. "What is it?"

Sleep was the best fucking time to show a woman how to feel everything sexuality had to offer. It was the only time their minds were so fully relaxed she'd be willing to try anything. When her head told her she could conquer the world and nothing could ever hurt her.

The fear was gone.

The lust was immense and my cock ached to sink balls deep in that ready and waiting pussy.

"It's a candle. I'm going to light the end, and no matter what I do to you, you can't come until the flame burns out," I said as I licked the back of her shoulder and she shivered in shock, eyes flew open and sought me out.

"What?" She was more alert now, but still thick with the haze I'd get to play with. "Jesus," she rushed out, and her breathing was heavy and raw as it sounded rough as it was dispelled from her throat.

"He isn't with us, love. But the devil sure as fuck is."

"You're sick," she breathes with raspy arousal. "So sick. So why does it feel so fucking good?"

"Because you're letting go. Are you ready, Soul Raiser?" I stoked a finger down her spine and she bucked, ass out in the air as she pulled herself higher onto her knees.

Perfect.

I gripped her hips and held her so tightly that I knew my bruises would show. The thought of her covered in my marks made my cock impossibly hard. "Stay on your knees, baby, I need to get to the main course."

Then I twisted, laid down on my back, and shimmied

myself between her silken thighs. "This right here, this is love. And I'm about to drown in it," I growled, right before I blindly lit the candle's wick then looked back up at Ophelia who was now above me, doggy style and with a look of lust blowing her eyes so wide, I wondered how they would ever un-dilate. "Remember, no coming until you can feel the burn, sweetheart. Be my good girl and do as you are told and you might just be rewarded."

Then I attacked. I licked and I teased, all until she was screaming and writhing above me. Riding my face and cutting off my air supply. She was shameless in taking what she needed and I was brutal in keeping it from her. I drew back and pinched her clit, she screamed into the room and slammed her hands down beside my head in frustration. Then I started all over again, circling where she needed me most with my index, working her into a state without sense, thick with confusion as to what she needed the most.

As to where she *needed* me the most.

The flat side of my tongue caressed her, lapping over her clit hidden between her folds, and only gave her enough to scream again, begging, screaming that she was needing more. "Fuck, fuck, fuck! I can't! I need more, I need more! Deeper baby, I need you deeper!" Her head was thrown back, face contorted in ecstasy, back arched and not an ounce of worry about how she may appear to me as my eyes burned into every part of her that I could see. I savored it, allowed it to slither beneath this strange skin of mine as I used her in a way which pushed her to lose full control and toe the lines of her limits.

"You turn me into such a dirty slut, Blake. You make me need it!" she cried in a high-pitched tone that came out breathless. The rhythm changed and she tried to bounce on my face instead, searching for the fingers that tormented her.

Naughty girl.

I stopped, pulled my tongue and my fingers away before I pinched her clit and spanked her ass, making her hiss. I could feel the burn run through her and straight into me. "Do you want me to beg?" she moaned. "Want me to be your good girl? Anything, I'd do anything. Just let me finish, Blake, *please,* just let me finish!" The neediness inside of her was like a dick pump and I grew in inches at the sound of her desperation.

I needed her.

I needed to torment her as much as I needed to be deep inside her.

I needed her beside me though more than I needed anything else. At this moment, I realized that I needed *her* more than I needed anything else.

"Do you think you could handle being my good girl and my filthy little slut, Ophelia? Do you think you can handle me at my worst, with whatever dark side of myself I wanted to show you?" I rasped, my breath cool against her hot, weeping core.

"Yes!" she exclaimed.

"Will you be standing beside me when I take another life, Soul Raiser? With your own freewill?"

"Yes! Yes, Blake. Fuck, yes. Okay? I promise. I'll be there. I'll see it all. I'll be your good, filthy little slut if you just make me come!"

Now she was frantic, so close to the edge of a crash so brutal from her high, she'd end up back in slumber before I was ready. I persisted forward and latched onto her core as I sank three fingers inside of her tight cunt without warning. A raw scream tore from her throat as a lone tear dropped onto my cheek with a splatter of her depraved satisfaction.

"Blake!" she chanted, the sound fucking musical as she found her comfort and began to bounce again. "I'm so full, it burns! Baby, it burns. It feels so good, so wrong. Why does it feel so fucking good when this is so fucking filthy and wrong?" she mumbled incoherently, an utter mess in her pleasure and I thrived on the state she was in. I pulled out at the exact same time I pulled the candle from her ass, lifted my shoulders and turned us.

She landed with a thud onto the mattress and in one swift move the candle was across the room, my position more accurate as I devoured her core and made her come all simultaneously with my actions. She was at mid-gasp when it hit her. When her body betrayed her and locked up so tightly, I thought she'd crack a bone. Solid as a rock, she convulsed as the wave of arousal coursed through her like an unrelenting wave of a tsunami.

At the peak of her high, I moved up her body and shucked off my jeans with one thought on my mind. In one savage hammer of my hips, I was inside of her. My head hung heavy as I groaned into her shoulder. Tingles consumed my entire body as I had to take a moment to settle. To breathe and not lose full control of the tender moment.

I had never felt anything so instantly euphoric.

Like ink in water, it sprawled through me quicker than thought as I was so close to the edge, the precipice was sticking its obnoxious tongue out at me. I flipped it off, then drew back, rutting into her with abandon.

Savage, brutal, fucking blissfully raw. I gave her my everything. I gave her my worst. I wrapped my hand around her throat until her eyes rolled back into her skull. The milky whites of elation stared back up at me as I pulled her seizing body into another orgasm and threw us both over the edge. "Good girls that follow orders get rewarded with the dick, Soul Raiser," I whispered into her ear as I filled her so wholly, I was writing my name on her womb.

This time, she bellowed.

Our shared release rollicked through her entire neighborhood.

Hell, I think we may have even woken the *dead*.

"Good girl, sweetheart. That's my good, good dirty fucking girl for coming for me like my good little whore."

CHAPTER
TEN

Ophelia
Control - Halsey

"Your aftercare is such a huge contradiction to your fucked up personality," I mumbled as Blake cleaned me up once again. I didn't know what got into me, but there was no going back now. I literally left my body and danced with the stars.

It is what it is, I guessed.

I was his for as long as he was here and I was over fighting it.

I liked being bad. Feeling dirty. Feeling praised. I liked it all.

It was mine and I'd fight like a vicious bitch if someone tried to take it from me.

He replaced all of my trepidation with excitement and now, I just wanted everything he was willing to give me. He took away all of my worries. With him being so fucked up, it gave me more room to be less than perfect in this more than *shown to be* perfect world and I knew that was what drew me in the most with this bad, bad man.

He caught me, tied me down, and crawled inside my head.

Now, there was no escaping him.

He lived there rent free.

"I take care of the things that I own, love, and you best believe I own you. Every sinful part of this body crafted from the arts," he mused slowly, transfixed as he ran a finger up my ribs, under the curve of my boob, and up between my sternum to place his hand over my heart. "Even the darkness that dwells in here. I see it, the curiosity, the depravity. I accept it because it's mine."

I blew out a breath and chuckled uneasily. "You see too much," I half-joked, baked from a hefty arousal that was still seeping from my body.

"I see everything," he countered. "As I said, the night is young and I have a kill list for us."

I got this feeling that he would save me from the downfall in whatever was to come next. I gave myself to him in every way possible and now I was following his lead, without asking questions. I'd follow him over the cliff itself if he asked me too. After all, this is way better than living without ever having lived at all. Because that's what we do, we go day to day never having stopped to ask ourselves what the catalyst of that very day was. What made our hearts race, our minds calm and our palms sweat? "Okay."

"Okay?" he parroted with a hiked brow like he didn't quite believe me. "No protest?"

"Would I win if there was?" I countered.

"Would you win against a serial killer you brought back from the dead and dreams of killing *with* you as much as he dreams of *fucking* you senseless?" he asked in question as he stared off into space as if he was actually thinking it over before he shrugged his shoulder and turned back to me. "Fuck no."

I rolled my eyes and smirked. "Well, there is a flaw in that plan, serial killer batman."

Both his eyebrows disappeared under his hairline. "Oh yeah, and what's that?"

"I can't feel my legs and my ass burns." I chuckled as I wrapped my legs around him and pulled him in close. My hands ran down the defined muscles of his bare, tanned back. He was a fucking god. Chiseled to perfection. Every curve and definition was sculpted just right and my mouth watered at the feel of him against me.

"I could always kiss away the aches?" he offered with a cocky smirk.

"Ixnay. That's what got us into this mess." I leaned forward and bit his lower lip, drawing it into my mouth before biting down and drawing blood. At the same time, I dug in my nails to draw artful lines of crimson silk across his shoulders.

"I have another confession," I whispered sweetly, sultry. "I like it rough too. Add blood to the mix? I'll come for you just from the taste."

He stared down at me with narrowed eyes and a little lift on the corner of his lips. He hissed and I let go of the bottom lip with a pop.

"Is that so?"

"Hmm-hmm," I mused dreamily, taking in everything before me with eyes that burned hot for him in a desire that could bring down this earth around us.

I could almost hear the crumble of it now.

"Prove it," he dared, as I locked my legs around the backs of him and flipped us so he was beneath me.

I reached into the bedside drawer and pulled out the pocket knife I kept there for safety and then reached down onto the floor for the candle. He held my hips to stop me from falling. Nabbing his lighter, I lit the bit that was left of the wick and smirked down at him. "Handle me if you can." I dared in return as I began to drop the hot wax over his naked chest. He hissed and groaned, his first reaction to curl in on himself but after a moment, he resisted and laid back down flat with a taunt in his dark eyes. A feral look on his face as he gritted his teeth so tightly, I could hear the brittleness of them from my throne across his lap.

"Soul Raiser," he growled, nostrils flared and face darkly fierce.

"Shh, baby. You wanted me to prove it, I'll prove it," I whispered back in a low seduction. "Wrist please."

He brought it to me tentatively, and I made a small gash across the tender flesh that parted like butter and bled so beautifully for me. Then I lowered my hand and burned him with the wax so the heat would be more intense. Red wax caked across his flesh, covering the expanse in crimson tears that harden against me, and every moan and hiss that tore from his throat had my clit throbbing and my tight channel fluttering. Then I brought his wrist to my mouth and licked away a line of blood from his wound as my entire body detonated like an explosion and rocked me to my core. I moaned and cried out to the room as I shivered and twitched above him from the rawness of the orgasm after so many other tender ones.

"I'll be dammed," he whispered in sexy approval. "My pretty little psycho. Guess the holy water failed both of us, huh?" That dark chuckle only added to the arousal I was leaking all over him.

I opened my feral eyes and gazed down at him with lust

consuming me. It burned so fucking hot. "Hmm-hmm." Was all I could manage as I came down from my high.

"My blood-thirsty temptress. Let's go paint the town red, baby. I found some real fuckers I think you're going to love watching me kill."

The funny thing was?

I no longer feared if he may be right.

CHAPTER
ELEVEN

Blake

Venom - Icon For Hire

As we walked down the street, I marveled at all of the Halloween decorations. From one property to the next, the dead consumed the lane. If only they knew that on such an unholy night the dead walked beside them. If they watched closely, they would see the shadows thrive and dance, twirling within the night, finally free to play on the devil's playground.

Oh, it was a wicked, wicked night alright and that was fucking beautiful.

They all thought Halloween itself was the night to fear.

How wrong the little people were.

It was the witching hour that should install terror in your hearts.

"Where are we going?" Ophelia whispered beside me. I side-eyed her, something sinister in my gaze as I smirked cruelly at her light-footedness and small voice.

"Well, Soul Raiser, I'm willing to bet that when you google searched my name, you also read how I died."

She stopped dead, blank eyes rolling to meet mine as the answer finally dawned on her. "You're going to kill the cop? The one who killed you?" she asked slowly, quizzically.

I didn't blame her.

This one wouldn't be easy.

But it sure as fuck would be thrilling.

"Sure am, darling."

"B-but..." she stammered.

"But what, love?"

"He's in prison." The look on her angelic face was comical.

Pupils were blown wide, a slight scarlet tint to her smooth cheeks, and those perfect fucking lips pouted beautifully in shock.

My cock ached to be between them again.

"And?" I taunted.

"And, how the fuck are we going to get in there? That is like the lamb waking in the dawn and being like *'oh hey farmer, no need for an escort. I'll just mosey on over and take myself to the slaughter',*" she flounders, hysterically. The fierce whisper of her voice was a clap of thunder in the dead of night.

I chuckled, nostril-flaring as I tried to restrain the outrageous laugh that wanted to tear free from my throat.

My soul raiser was as endearing as she was stunning.

"But that's the fun of it, is it not?"

"Dude, you're dead. I'd get locked up and committed to some psycho ward for the warped shit you're about to do. As much as I'm down to spend a night playing with murderous sin, I will not be your fool and I will not take the heat for a crime I'm not committing... Well, not *actively* committing." She frowned as she thought over those words.

My face turned cold, and serious, while I stepped toward her. She swallowed thickly, her throat working as her entire body tensed. As I stalked her, a predator with his pretty prey, I slowly lifted my hand to remove a loose strand of her hair and tucked it behind her ear. "Don't insult me, love. I would never allow anything to harm you." The raspy husk of my voice was deep, raw, and dropped twelve octaves as the wind around us turned to ice.

The air thickened, and despite my encouraging words, the feeling of malice to them was evident. I didn't like being questioned and I sure as fuck didn't like my woman thinking I'd allow anything in this shitpit of a stain called world harm her.

I'd burn the entirety of this planet and take her with me before that ever happened.

She cleared her throat, and I removed my hand from her cheek, dropped it to her neck, and stroked the tender flesh there before collaring her gently. When her eyes fluttered, I closed my grip and yanked her toward me, putting pressure on her windpipe. She mewled, and a sultry groan whispered past her lips as her arousal wafted through the air at my rough hold on her.

"Do you trust me, Soul Raiser? I'd think very carefully about that answer, sugar."

She nodded and I knew exactly what she was doing, like her pussy bouncing on my dick, she was thrusting her throat into my palm for the same feeling of the pressure she chased. "Good girl. Now come here." I pulled her into me more forcefully, my lips fused with hers.

Rough and raw I made her feel every part of me.

Here, cloaked within the darkness, surrounded by the decorations of the dead, I laid claim to the most silken lips I had ever felt. A circuit of white trash bags, rigged to look like dancing little girls in billowing gowns, stood in a circle like a merry-go-round, started to shriek and sing a very warped-sounding nursery rhyme.

You're my addiction.
Dizzy ever since I cut off your lips
Welcome To All Hallows' Eve
We're going to steal all of your magic
Ashes to ashes, knife to bone
Don't knock here, the Candyman is home.
Ready to eat and devour, that glorious fucking soul.

The cackle that followed that chilling tune had me frowning. I knew people liked to win the creepy factor on Halloween, but what the fuck was that?

"Fuck," Ophelia exclaimed as she pulled back in fright. "Jesus. That is the most fucked up thing I've ever heard. Kids walk past here for fuck's sake. What are they playing out threatening to cut off their lips and eat their souls?"

Couldn't say I disagreed with her thought process. With a shrug, I turned to face her. "Wait here." Then I stalked toward the house and right through the door of the garage.

When I reemerged, it was with a strike of luck. Gas can in one hand, a box of matches in the other, and a goofy grin on my face. I lumbered back over to a smug-looking Ophelia. "Not the worst idea you've had tonight." She chuckled.

"Want to do the honors?" I asked, wondering how far my hand of corruption had brought her. She stared at me for a moment and when she didn't respond, I began to soak the display in gasoline. When I was done and the weird-looking things looked like drowned mice, I struck a match and held it before me. A delicate hand wrapped around my wrist and I looked down to see Ophelia standing beside me, looking down at the display and I knew it was a silent acceptance.

We'd do this together.

I wouldn't push for more.

So as one, we tossed the match and stepped away as the entire lawn went up in flames. My dark eyes danced with the hue of orange and blue fire. The heat licked against my cool skin and I smirked while we stood over the ruins. The fire was such a beautiful thing.

Deadly too. A little like my Soul Raiser.

I guessed you could even say a little like my infatuation with her too.

Because burning some shitty little Halloween display was the least I would do when something displeased her.

A shrill cry came from the direction of the house and we both turned toward it. Panic started to creep into her stunning emeralds and I placed my hands on her hips and pulled her back into me.

"We have to make sure the fire doesn't spread," she whispered.

"Glen!" a woman screamed. "Glen, wake up, I smell smoke!" Then there was a commotion and loud footsteps could be heard thundering toward the door.

"I think they have it covered, love," I murmured in her ear and delighted in the shiver that skated down her spine.

"We should run," she purred. Apparently, the fire also got her hot in other areas and I was more than happy to splash my load to help contain the wildfire that brewed in her core right before my very eyes.

"That, I think I have covered." I smirked as I held her

closer and allowed the darkness to conceal us, stealing us from space and time as it spat us out in the Valley Of The Corrupt. Ophelia stumbled from my arms, disoriented and I loved knowing that I could still surprise her.

"What the fuck?" she drawled drowsily as she spun in a circle. She shuddered as if somebody had just walked over her grave and I smirked wider. "Where are we? How did we get here?"

"Outside the prison, darling. And I'm dead, remember? I have special gifts." I winked and she frowned, brows furrowed with a glare that could scorch.

"Any other tricks up your sleeves? You know, besides teleporting and walking through damn doors." The hiss was low, but I could tell her shock was waning.

"That would be telling now, wouldn't it? Stick around to find out what's next." When I wink at her again, she huffed and rolled her eyes which made me chuckle.

Then she straightened, stared at the prison in the distance lost to the baleful clouds of darkness, then turned back to face me with refusal on her face. "No fucking way. You are not doing that weird ghostly thing to me again. No *fucking* way. And in a prison? Are you nuts? We would get caught!" she flurried, frustrated with my plan, and when my face fell firm, she drew her head back and scoffed. "Yes, I trust you. No, I don't wish to puke," she added and I grunted in amusement. "Can't you just... I don't know. Like, bring him out here?" Her brows danced as she screwed up her face.

"I could, but that would be boring. I don't do boring. I do exciting. Besides..." I stalked toward her, my features the features of death coming to claim your soul, then fisted my hand into her dark locks at the crown of her head and pulled back while I rasped, "I'm going to slaughter anyone I please. I'm going to paint the scene in my wicked art and then I'm going to fuck you in the pretty crimson, sweetheart. And when I do all of that..." I leaned forward slightly, my lips brushed hers and she quivered in anticipation. "It will be far from fucking boring." Then I let go and stepped away, allowing her to pant after me in sweet desperation.

CHAPTER
TWELVE

Ophelia
High - Zella Day

There was a tinge of hell-fire red in the pitch-black daunting skies above us. The stunning hues entwined into an ominous concoction and it had the thrill of a deadly kind of excitement rush down my spine. It was stunning, magnificent even, as it exuded a creepy, hollow feeling to the trepidation that surrounded it. Given the time, there should be nothing but darkness above us. The red hues, a nod from the man downstairs I guessed. The prison was dark, concealed in a frightful looking night and quiet away into the distance. My heart pounded brutally in my chest as the nerves in my stomach fluttered like the wild wings of a raven.

I was terrified.

What he asked me to do, exceeded my quota of some naive, blood-thirsty fun.

I closed my eyes and stared at the ground. As I licked my lips, I tried to calm the buzz that was fierce inside my ears.

The thump of my pulse that hammered beneath my skin. But nothing I was doing worked. The world around me began to fade as my panic attack wrapped me in its cocoon. Blake stepped forward and wrapped his arms around me. The second his skin touched mine, the hard shell that was engulfing me dissipated, retracted by the ice of his touch and I could finally breathe again.

"Breathe, Soul Raiser," he whispered and the husked vibration of his tone trembled down the side of my throat. "I got you."

The dizziness made my eyes swim and my stomach sink, but I could finally see what was in front of me. Blake had moved around to my front, a soft caress smoothed along my nape as he massaged away the tender ache from my worry.

"I promise, you'll love this as soon as we walk out of there unseen. The thrill, baby? It's a damn rush you'll start to crave," he gushed, a wicked smirk of twisted joy on his thick lips.

"I think it's a dead man I'm starting to crave," I whispered to the wind, hoping the breeze would swallow it whole.

But he heard me. Because he hears everything.

"Good, because I have no intention of ever letting you go."

Those words should have scared me.

If I was paying attention instead of drowning within his dark and harrowing gaze, I would have been.

"Ready?" he asked and I nodded as I heaved a deep breath and held it hostage within my lungs.

I stepped into him and he consumed me, moving me through the fibers of time and when the darkness receded, I was standing behind warped iron bars as I looked back out into the prison from the inside. I gazed at rows, upon rows of cells, stacked higher than the tallest mountain.

Dirty clouds tinged into a brown, murky shadow rose high from the ground and I recoiled at how haunted it looked. What I was expecting a prison to look like, I didn't know. But one straight out of a damn horror movie wasn't it.

"What's the matter, Soul Raiser? Not what you expected?" he whispered and I shuddered as his cool breath tickled against the curve of my throat.

"Not at all," I murmured back, my whisper just as low as his.

The cell we were standing in was on a high level, the communal area below lost to an abyss. The silence was eerie, not a prisoner was awake and that seemed more chilling than the fact that I was surrounded by the worst of the worst of human society. The Valley Of The Corrupt was a high-security prison about two hundred miles away from Black Wood back in Hallows Point. The closest prison to us and the only one that housed the vilest and most malevolent, diabolic human beings to walk this earth.

I cleared my throat to shuck away the unease when a nasally snort sounded behind me and I jumped out of my skin. Blake pressed my back to his chest as he curved his palm across my mouth in order to stifle my scream. A man, unkept, large in size with a rounded belly laid on his back with a leg overhung on the metal framed bed, snoring to the damn lions with the sound that crackled throughout the cell, sound asleep without any hint that we were here lingering above him.

Fuck, my heart just ran away.

Probably back to find my fucking sanity.

I heaved, my shoulders rose with each ragged breath.

Then I convulsed as I jittered in his firm hold when his other hand trailed down my chest and settled at my core. "How about it, love?" he rasped, as he flexed his grip while he cupped my heated pussy. "You have been such a good little brat following all of my orders. Do you think you could follow one more?" I trembled, arousal spiked in my veins as my skin warmed to the touch of an inferno. "Answer me, Soul Raiser." I nodded, humming yes into his palm. "Good, then be quiet." He removed his hand and wrapped it around my throat, his other hand delving under the waistline of my pants.

First, he bypassed where I needed him most.

Where I *ached* for him most.

Then trailed a feathered caress across the top of my inner thigh and I squirmed and almost darted to the other side of the cell in order to escape the overwhelming sensation to my senses. He pulled me back into him with the heel of his palm on my pelvis and I tried my hardest to settle into his stellar touch. A mewl crept into the back of my throat and I had to settle for releasing it within the walls of my mind instead. My head lolled on his shoulder, and a cloud of contentment fell around me.

He hummed into my ear and I could have sworn it sounded like...

We're gonna kill tonight.

Moonlight, blood shine.

We're gonna kill tonight.

Fuck, fuck, fuck all throughout the night.

My eyebrows hit my hairline at the lack of marbles in this man's head. "You're insane, aren't you?" I whispered in bewilderment. "Your killer anthem?"

"Certifiably so, and yes. Now hush," he murmured just as a barely there-to-the-touch skimmed across my folds and I shook in his arms. It was on my lips to plead with him, to beg him to give me more.

I knew what he wanted, I knew what he *needed* and it was utter submission.

I just wasn't in the mood to give it to him.

I wanted to feel that high and I was going to force him to give it to me.

"Blake," I rasped in a sultry tone that had him tensing behind me. "Give it to me, or I'll give it to myself." With him, I felt like I had found my voice. I was more open, more in touch with my needs and I was even bold enough to demand them.

His hand tightened threateningly around my throat and I smirked, grinding my ass back into his groin, the thickness there was an incentive to rock even harder. "That isn't being quiet now, is it? Do you want this disgusting, vile cunt to wake up and watch me do these dirty, sinful things to you, love?" he growled and the thought of him getting angry that I might say yes to that was a massive turn-on. "Because I assure you, I'd burn out his eyes first." I moaned, my heart frantic and my core soaked. "His ears would be next." I never had the time to prepare, to process, before the teasing stopped and he thrusted three thick and dirtily skilled fingers inside of me. Just as I gasped he clamped his hand over my mouth once more and captured my wanton sounds with his hefty palm. "Because even your sounds are mine, Soul Raiser."

Fuck, I think my soul just left my body.

The penetration was what I needed. What I craved and when he gave it to me, everything else came crashing to the forefront. This man, this creature from beyond the veil of life was an entity thriving within my veins. I could feel him everywhere, a drug that melted my inhibitions and took away my tortuous thoughts. With Blake, there was no line to toe of a normal society, there was no ache in my heart at another dreadful day dawning.

He gave me purpose.

He gave me lust and right now, he gave me the overwhelming urge to come.

Just like this prison, my mind was quiet and I felt like I was drifting through still waters, the coolness against my skin. "Do it," I rasped as I flexed, rocking my cunt against his thick fingers as my clit searched for his palm. "Make me feel cold, baby. Give me a taste of death."

"Patience, love," he murmured into my ear. "Only good girls get to come." Then he pulled out and spun me around. "Only good girls get this dick too."

I stared at him in outrage as my defiance got the better of me. Edging, so sinfully wicked, had me riled up and ready to feel the flames. I trailed my deft finger along my collarbone, down the curve of my breasts, and right to my cunt. I was hot, burning with a need that ached. As I found my clit, he smirked at me. As he leaned against the bars of the cell, a malicious look of deviance on his face, I narrowed my eyes but continued anyway, because that was a look that had me about to sail the precipice. I thrust my unskilled—unskilled compared to his—fingers inside of me and circled my clit with my other hand. I moaned and rocked, my skin on fire from the arousal that had me needing to scream my release. Fuck, I'd never needed to scream as badly as I needed to scream now. The moments of our depraved time together are a slideshow in my mind as I remember the priest, the confessional, and the wake-up call when he fucked me senseless. My mind was a riot and my libido was a buck trying to throw me from its back like a cowgirl.

But I couldn't.

There is no way I'd scream for the animals around us.

The monsters I could feel looming within the shadows.

Instead, I bit my lip and clenched my eyes closed. Because I was there, ready to dive head first from that cliff and the excitement that Blake was watching, that the man who slept mere feet away from us would never know, had the sweet taste of salvation pooling within my mouth.

My pussy clenched and fluttered and the sultry moan built in my throat, then suddenly, everything was gone.

My fingers, my palm. The peak that was screaming for me to return and jump that last hill into bliss. My back was flat against a cold cement wall, my arms pinned above my head and my wrists clasped in a large hand. Tears welled in my eyes and the urge to scream was so much more forceful, a sob bubbled, and just as I allowed it to escape, that damn hand—the one that now smelled thickly of my arousal—was back over my mouth, capturing my sounds once more.

"Careful now, love. Dead men don't play nice. You'll come—oh how sweetly you *will* come for me—as soon as you can learn to be my good girl again. Follow my orders. Do you understand that, baby? That your pleasure is mine?" Blake rasped against my lips and the coolness of his breath stroked against them in a damned caress and I shuddered. "Answer me, sugar. Let me hear those words."

I nodded, and the first tear fell as I opened my eyes to meet his. "I think... I think I don't hate you anymore," I whispered and that was my greatest sin—my greatest confession—of them all.

I was falling in love with a monster and that made me never want to feel the love of a saint ever again.

I just couldn't say that yet. I never knew how.

"That's okay, baby. The good ones who're secretly bad

normally do." Then he kissed me and a kaleidoscope of colors burst behind my eyes. I groaned into his mouth, my tongue dueling for dominance with his and ultimately submitting to his power.

I was a victim of my desire and I'd be lying if he said he never played me perfectly.

"Now, should I rise from the dead so we can have a little bit of fun?" he groaned with restraint as he pulled away, his forehead resting against mine as his breathing grew heavy.

I hummed, needier than ever to give him exactly what he wanted, and truth be told...

I wanted it too.

CHAPTER THIRTEEN

Blake
Back From The Dead - Halestorm

I leaned over Dale Rogers. The pig of a man slept like a slitherine before me and it made me curl my lip in distaste. I could still smell Ophelia. Her arousal was thick in the air and for the first time in my life—*undead* life —I found myself wanting to get this over with. The kill was no longer as sweet as the scent on her skin.

The scent that was one hundred percent all of her.

Tonight was supposed to be a night of mayhem and murder and all my killer heart wanted to do again was to sink balls deep inside of her smooth and tight pussy. Even if she was being bratty right now. I needed her more than I needed control. I needed her taste, her scent, the feel of her skin against mine.

After all, I assumed I never had long left.

What was normal about coming back from the dead and what rules applied?

I growled. I couldn't think about that right now.

Right now, I needed to play.

I took my switchblade and shoved it up Dale's nose, one nostril at a time then looked back to a heaving Ophelia who stood concealed within the shadows with eyes that watched my every move, eyes that saw everything. "The smell of you, is all mine too, Soul Raiser. *All* fucking mine."

When Dale's eyes shot open and he opened his mouth to scream, I smirked and shoved the blade down his throat and throat fucked him with it. "Hey, mate. Long time, not dead right?" I whispered in a sinister chuckle and the whites of his eyes burst, the shock-horror made his pupils shrivel. I threw my head back, and the laugh twisted as I thrived on that look. Confusion consumed him and I toyed with it, playing him like a fiddle to my blade as I painted it cherry fucking red.

"Do you remember? All of the sick things you did to me?" I asked as I hummed lowly because I sure as fuck did. My dark eyes turned toward Ophelia. "Could use a little help, love."

She prowled from the shadows like a sultry angel of death and Dale tried to turn his head, the head burning with pain to see who I was speaking to, but I pushed the knife in harder and refused to let him utter one sick and vile word. "Hold his arms," I demanded. Once she stood behind him, still lost to the darkness within this shittily-lit cell, I carved out his tongue and pulled it from his rotten mouth. Lifting it to eye level, I examined it. "They feel a lot rougher when cut from the mouth, Soul Raiser. Want to feel it?" I teased and I could hear her mock gag through the whispers of the cell and I chuckled even louder. "Fair enough." Then I tossed the worthless thing behind me. He wouldn't need it and now for anyone who woke, he would sound like a slobbering mess.

Either a cunt feeling the sorrow of his sins or in this place, more than likely a cunt that needed to cry just to finish in his palm. "Perfect," I mused as I pulled away and got to my knees beside him. "Two pounds of flesh for every pound you took of mine?" I questioned as he shook his head frantically. Blood ran in rivers from his mouth. He now looked like a clown with a tongue of blood painted on his chin.

I dug that.

The nasal septum was gone, torn to shreds so all that remained was a huge gaping hole that looked like a gateway to a void of Hell, because you couldn't see shit through the shadows of blood that gushed from it. Fucker should have known better than to dare smell my woman.

Asshole.

"Did it hurt?" Ophelia asked in the hush of night and I retained my attention on bringing Dale's arm out and away from her so I could carve him up. I wasn't interested in the poetics tonight. I just wanted blood.

Revenge.

Peace.

I didn't look at her, didn't need to. I knew what she was asking. "Don't remember a thing, darling."

Nothing more needed to be said as I dug in my knife and curved it under the surface of his flesh. He cried out, the sound nothing but a horrific, wet gurgle that bubbled from his shredded throat and splattered against my face in little speckles of his plasma. I licked my lips and pulled away the first layer of his skin.

"See, baby, see how pretty it can be?" I mused as I looked at the creamy flesh that on one side looked like it belonged to a hobo, but was still somewhat bright and smooth. Yet, on the other side, a wall of risen bumps and rotten flesh curdled.

"This shouldn't fascinate me," Ophelia uttered. I groaned as my eyes rolled back in my head as her breath feathered against me. "Yet it does. You've never looked as sexy as you do covered in red."

"Death is life, sweetheart. We fear it without ever having understood it. We're no different from the curious minds of a mortician. Only our subjects are alive." I winked at her and she shook her head.

"How do you do that? How do you make murder seem so normal?"

I shrugged a smug look on my crooked lips. "It's a gift," I mused.

Dale's eyes rolled back and the shift in them told me that he saw *her*. My woman stood above him as a veil of darkness. I slashed out and butchered his eyes in a vicious snarl that flew from me in a sprayed arch of spittle. The sound could rival any beast in the wild protecting its mate. But I was worse than a wild animal.

I was worse than the worst.

I was the unburdened.

I cared not for the atrocious acts I committed.

The only thing I would ever think twice about was the victim under my blade.

If they deserved it, I'd quite happily serve it.

With a sadist smile and a big fuck you.

I got so consumed in my bloodlust, that I hadn't noticed the damage until it was too late. Just as I feared with the priest, the darkness stole me from the murky gray light of my senses when it came to this bastard looking at what was good and what was all fucking mine. I knew it was subjective, drastic. But she was all that I had and I wanted to keep her to myself.

I brutalized him in a way words would never describe. When I was done, heaving and thriving for every breath, I looked up to see Ophelia.

She stepped forward, mouth open as sweet, sexual pants of arousal puffed from her open mouth. Her eyes were wide and filled with the ecstasy of a woman that felt the desire and knew what it was like to feel desired. She was covered, a mirror image of myself as blood artfully painted her face. I stood to my feet, in a rush to get to her.

To *feel* her.

I needed her right now. More than I needed another kill.

One hand slithered between the strands of her hair, the other landed on her hip as I lifted her from the ground and hiked her thighs around my waist. As I turned, I backed us up against the cell wall and spread her thighs, I grew weak at the knees. There was no foreplay, no pretense as I removed her pants and thrust myself inside of her, sheathed to the hilt as I let out a roar that woke every prisoner within this cell block. Like a man unleashed, I rutted against her with wild abandon and strived for the end we both craved.

Fuck punishment. I needed her so fucking badly, that it would have brought a lesser man to tears.

"You're so fucking beautiful, Ophelia. So fucking perfect," I exclaimed in a breathy whisper into her ear.

The cell block was crazed, rioting beyond their bars and shouting their jest at whatever they thought was happening within this cell. I kissed her, consumed her, and stole every purr and whimper for myself.

"You have been more than a good girl for me, my love.

So fucking fuckable painted red. Come! Come, baby, fucking come and cover my cock when you do!"

Every light within the cell block flickered on and faltered. It was a mass of supercharged static electricity and short circuits.

Nobody heard her.

Nobody heard me.

In fact, nobody knew we were here at all.

CHAPTER
FOURTEEN

Ophelia
Parasite Eve - Bring Me The Horizon

My mind was screaming, my chest pumping, and everything inside of me rioted at the feel of him moving inside of me. He was rooted so deep that I could feel his essence as it crept throughout my entire body and lit it up from the inside out. I was hot, too hot and that was what I needed from him most. To give me a feel of the in-between and take away all of my senses. I wanted to toe the line and feel more connected to him than I have ever felt connected to anyone. I burned alive under the infliction, but my heart remained cold and fresh like the breath of a peppermint.

An ancient kiss that pulled my soul back and forth.

This man took me to new heights, ones that far exceeded beyond the astral plane and I was struggling *not* to melt under the infliction of the raw sensations coursing through me. That was when he touched me in the way he first ever touched me. The coldness of his hand seeped through the inferno on my skin and chilled me to my soul.

I felt cold, and that felt like a cocoon of content. Like when you laid idle in a warm bath for too long that when it turned to that crisp sensation circling you, you couldn't help but lay back for a few moments longer.

I craved that.

The lightness that came with it.

"I need you, Soul Raiser," he whispered into my ear and my heart ceased beating altogether. "You make me a bad man and that, love, is saying something. All I ever knew before you was evil."

"They brand evil as something sinister, you have shown me that evil is the tool we need to fight the demons from the worst parts of Hell. You are what this world needs, and if I had to summon you all over again, I would," I whispered back before biting the lobe of his ear with a wanton moan.

What a warped conception of murder.

He groaned. Head rested on the curve of my ample breasts as he kneaded into me and I smiled while I ran my fingers through his dark hair. Once we finished, just as the cell block was in an uproar, he carried me through the walls once more and out into the cool night's air. He was still dressed as he was when I summoned him.

Shirtless chest, glorious tattoos, and bare toes.

He was stunning. A darker contrast to the already dark night.

Only now, he was bathed in blood.

More blood, than the first second I ever laid eyes on him.

"I feel a little crazy," I admitted, suddenly shy of everything I'd done and witnessed.

Everything *we* had done.

How quickly my researcher's heart became corrupt.

"Shy doesn't look good on you, sweetheart," he mused with a smirk. "Wickedry sure as fuck does." As he swiped the back of his leather jacket across his mouth, I became transfixed.

I cleared my throat and walked a few steps ahead of him, needing to find the air to breathe again after being so consumed by him in every single aspect of my soul. I had never intended for this man to burrow so deep, and truthfully, I was still unsure how he had. "So, what's next on this trick-or-treat murder tour?" I asked as I tilted my head back and stared up at the moon. A gust of wind blew by and heightened the scent of copper in the air.

I spun on him when silence fell. He stared back at me, eyes cold and head hung with a tilt of his ominous lock of hair, and then just when I thought I'd never breathe again, he smiled at me. "You ever tasted ass?" he questioned and I narrowed my eyes on him in confusion. "Beefy, hairy, or not? Ever sank your teeth into some sweetly bitter flesh?"

"That. Is. Vile. *No*, of course, I haven't," I enunciated in disgust.

His smile grew wider. "Good. I bet it doesn't taste all that great."

"Was there a point to that horrifying question?"

"Always," he deadpanned.

"Which is?"

"Facts."

"Being?"

"Arse is nasty if it's dead."

Fucking hell, my head is spun on the wheels of weaving wool.

I'm a spider web of what in the ever-loving fuck was he saying right now. My mind went to dark places of his darkest sin and I wondered if he'd try and get me to eat somebody tonight. Because that was enough to make me run back toward the senses that seemed to leave me long, long ago. Right along with my damned marbles.

"I promised you tonight I'd show you the worst of the worst. So the next stop is the *cannibal cafe*."

"Cannibal what now?"

He chuckled darkly and I suddenly feared what I could be walking into next. "When I was scrolling the Net, you know, finding new victims and all that, I came across a cannibal. One in Hallows Point. He got released from county not too long ago."

"Fuck off," I scoffed. "No way is there a cannibal in Hallows Point, let alone Blackwood, those aren't a common thing you know. Like an atheist and a hippie." I shook my head and rolled my eyes.

Like fuck.

When he never shared in my humor, my face fell. "Are you serious?"

"Yep. As serious as the dead." He winked and I gulped.

Ew.

That was the most disgusting thing I'd ever heard.

Did I want to walk into the flesh den of a maniac?

No.

Did I want Blake to cleanse him from this world?

Yes.

Dilemma. Dilemma.

"Okay, I'm down." I shrugged with a pout after much-needed and careful consideration. He laughed at me and I glared at him. This took precious moments of my time to make this decision.

After all, what else would I be doing tonight?

Writing about the dead instead of fucking them.

Fuck.

No.

Double ew!

I couldn't think like that either.

There was no good way to describe how fucked up tonight had been.

"Okay, naughty girl. Let's go stalk a stalker," he grumbled as he reached for me.

"What do you mean?" I asked with hesitancy.

"He's on the prowl, so we need to go save a life before we take one, pretty girl."

"How do you know that?" At every turn, he had some warped, new superpower.

"I'm dead, sugar. I know everything."

So he kept telling me.

CHAPTER
FIFTEEN

Blake

Appetite for Destruction - Vo Williams

Tonight was *summoning* up to be better than any night I spent alive on this earth.

My good girl was so compliant, so greedy to know more, to give in to the warped curiosity of bloody mutilation. It was perfection and I couldn't have been more thankful to this All Hallows' Eve for gifting me with this pretty new pet who bent so easily to my will.

I saw the trepidation, the uncertainty, but it was nothing more than a glimmer in her dark emeralds as she said yes to everything I had to offer.

It was intoxicating.

Exhilarating.

I stood against the brick wall, a bare foot kicked up behind me as I chilled in the shadows. Ophelia danced on the balls of her feet with tapping fingers as her anticipation grew. I sucked my teeth, bored of waiting for this man to show his face as a trash can fell over down the alley and clattered throughout the night. Ophelia squealed and I smirked, deciding it would be fun to watch her pretty face contort into one of shock horror once again.

That moment of no restraint was pure euphoria. It was unbridled and unkept. It was a moment when you got to see the face of a person that was without the burden of their mind.

Left with only instinct and without inhibitions.

It was the first insight into the soul without ripping it from the human body.

Oh how fucking stunning she wore that look.

As she turned to stare behind her, I cracked my neck and changed my face, letting the skeletal man out to play. The flesh on the left side of my face dissipated into milky ash, exposing bone while the right side stayed bright and intact. Ophelia was clutching her chest when she turned back to face me as I singsonged, "*Boo*." She screamed, jumping in the air only for me to catch her and spin us until her back is pressed firmly into the cool bricks.

"You evil little prick," she hissed and I licked my lips ready to kiss away the sin on her own.

"Evil, yes. Little prick? I think not," I groaned as I rocked my very large prick into her groin and she purred, head thrown back to expose her slender throat as her back chafed against the wall.

I nibbled on the tender column where her neck met the shoulder, drawing her sweet flesh into my mouth as she chuckled.

"You don't get to be sexy and an asshole," she uttered, then snapped her teeth at me in a sweet and desirable little pout. "That just isn't fair to mankind."

"But that is exactly what I am. A sexy asshole," I

corrected and chuckled when she scowled at me. I bit her lip, letting it go with a pop just as another mewl of arousal slipped past her parted lips. "And who gives a shit about mankind?"

As we stood there, under the veil of the giving night, the heavens opened and doused us in the rain of a world that would never be cleansed. I lost myself there, surrounded by the environment, the mood that was sensual, and within the eyes of a green sea that pulled me under its unforgiving current.

Something changed. Dead or alive, I was a man with the air of emotion that followed you everywhere.

An emotion that took root in your core and sprawled high inside of you until it reached that hollow part of your chest and set free the tiny ravens that fluttered wildly there.

It was a sensation I couldn't name.

Because whatever it was, it was indescribable.

And when a phoenix rises, greater than those ravens ferociously in my core, I knew that we were in trouble.

That *I* was in trouble.

Slowly, I lifted my hand and stroked her cheek in a gentle caress, memorizing every inch of her beauty that was without comparison. The silken strands turned slick, stuck to the side of her angelic face as water coiled on her long and dark lashes.

"Middle of the Night" by Elley Duhé played on the fine vines of the wind, an ultimate instrument that rivaled all others. As soon as I thought about it, the universe played it for us.

Being dead wasn't all that bad. It did come with some perks.

I stepped back, my hand fell from her cheek, down her

arm until I reached her wrist and took her hand in mine, then I pulled her with me. It would have chilled me had I not already been so cold.

I blinked through the rain, the cool water seeping through our clothes. My chest was bare and glistened under the dim lighting as the beaded drops ran in rivulets down my abs.

She looked back up at me with the largest doe-eyes I had ever seen. So much spiraled within them, whirling before me like the ticking of hypnosis I couldn't escape. A small smile spread across her thick and plump lips as I spun her, dancing under the world's sprinkled tears. The stars were beautiful as I held her close, moving as one, never taking my eyes from hers. I gave a part of myself to her at that moment that I had never given to anyone.

I suddenly became desperate, the need to crawl inside of her and become her very essence an urge stronger than the one to kill.

I needed everything this woman could give me and then some. I needed the air she breathed and the eyes she saw this warped world through. I needed her mind, her delicate caress.

I needed to consume her.

To feel her from the inside out.

"I can't stop," I growled as I pulled her into me even closer, my palm spread in the center of her spine. "I can't stop until I have it all. I can't stop until you give it to me." I lifted my free hand and placed it on her chest, right over her heart.

"Give what to you?" she breathed and her warm breath fanned across my tender skin like a silken feather.

I shuddered, closing my eyes and inhaling a calming

breath but I was almost feral with the need to claim it. To steal it from her.

"All of it. Your mind and your soul. Your heart and your..." I trailed off, my hold on her tightening as if I couldn't get enough. That if I didn't get enough something wild would burst free from my skin and get what it craved in a way I couldn't. My hand flexed, and her heart beat steadily under my palm. "Your love."

Ophelia's lashes fluttered, the pulse in her throat beat a pattern my eyes couldn't look away from. "I just need it all and I feel like I'd kill to get it. You make me a dangerous man, Ophelia. I'm not sure I can ever let you go."

We gazed at each other, a severity in my stare when the night fell silent. Tender moments passed, and nothing other than our heavy breathing slowly filled the space between us. Then suddenly another noise captured our attention and the moment of intense intimacy broke apart like the splintering of a tree under an axe.

Ophelia drew back, moving to look around me as I turned at the hip, staring over my shoulder and out of the mouth of the alley. A harrowing anguish-filled shriek bellowed around us and Ophelia pushed against my chest to move me backward. I stumbled, brows furrowed as I followed her around the corner. A woman had her cheek bashed into the brick. Blood splattered, darkening the already red stones as she thrashed wildly, kicking her legs and screaming bloody murder as she fought off a man three times her dainty size. Ophelia was already moving, but I hung back to watch with curiosity. The woman crab crawled along the ground, scrapes opening tender wounds in her arms as she bled. My brows arched in amusement.

Chick was a fighter.

She lifted her knee and kicked the fucker in the face, he flew backward and with a snarl of grievance, threw himself at her with redoubled brutality. Both hands fisted her hair, above her ear as he lifted her from the ground and smashed her head back into the paved sidewalk.

Knocked her out cold.

"Dumb bitch," he groused just as Ophelia prowled closer behind him.

"Dumb cunt," she hissed, drawing his attention and when he turned to see who was standing over his shoulder, she pivoted on her back foot, turned to the side with mastered skill, and side-kicked him around the face.

A tooth flew from his bloodied mouth and I hissed in real shock and a hell of a lot of excitement. "Hot damn, baby," I encouraged, cheering her on with the thriving need to see more blood be spilled.

"Why do men take what we never want to give?" she questioned with venom. "I mean, can you blame her for not wanting your toxic fucking touch burned into her skin? You're pathetic. Less than pathetic because being pathetic, means you were worth more than being a loser. But you?" Her tone turned low, calm, and fucking deadly. She drew out every word and I bulked in shock at this bad bitch side of her.

I fucking *loved* it.

Holy shit.

My woman was a fighter for justice all on her own.

She just dished it out with sexy as fuck combat.

"You're worthless. A stain on this earth and not a single tear would be shed if you ran back to the gutter you crawled out from," she finished.

He blinked, now the one crab crawling away as he tried

to regain his senses from the shock of her kicking them right out of his skull.

"Get up, try it with a girl that will fight back," she challenged. "I fucking *dare* you." Naturally, she had to throw in a hot as fuck taunt to boot.

One he couldn't resist.

He stumbled to his feet and shakily brought up his fists. I straighten, ready to intervene when he charged for her but she just danced like a ninja and I was struck a little too dumb to do anything other than stare at her. She kept her guard as she twirled around him like a boxer, making him chase her.

He fell forward when she leaned back.

It was a form of fucking art and I was pissed I had no idea it was one she knew.

When he struck, she swatted away his incoming fist like it was a nuisance and then countered when his guard was down with a swinging right hook. He spun and when he came full circle, she ran into a high kick, accompanied by a roundhouse that brought him to his knees.

This thing... this infatuation I had with this woman had grown into a full borderline obsession. I was salivating and ready to learn everything she had to show me. This was a night of horror and she turned it into a deadly kind of passion. In this life, or the next, I'd make this woman mine and I'd never let fucking go.

I was addicted.

With no intention of ever becoming sober.

Fuck that and handing over my happy pills.

They were mine.

She was mine.

"I think I should take away what you don't deserve."

She smirked, with her middle finger weaving in front of his dazed face.

He wobbled back and forth. Ophelia gave him a moment to come to and just when he uttered, "Fucking cunt!" And tried to grab her again with flaying hands. She knocked them away and swiftly brought up her right knee, shattered his nose, and sent him into the land of fucked-up dreams.

"Knife," she demanded and I laid it in her open palm as she stared down at him in disgust. She fell to one knee and stabbed him over and over again in his cock with a vengeance only a woman could house.

Demonic.

Only women could be demonic.

The denim of his blue jeans grew with a wet stain of blood that drizzled down his leg and onto the street beneath him. The sounds of moist flesh smacking together encroached around me and I shuddered.

As tall, burly, and murderous as I am, I spun and heaved at the sight. My own cock throbbing from the phantom ache of what I just witnessed. I cupped myself, whispering, "It's okay, bud. She loves our cock."

"Are you talking to yourself?" she questioned with an exhausted sigh sounding all sweet and shit at my back. Her warm breath feathered across my nape and I almost squealed like a fucking bitch myself as I turned around to see her swiping the back of her hand across her sweaty forehead removing a wet strand of hair. Blood ran in streams as it hurried down the sidewalk. Crimson puddles surrounded us as she left him there to bleed out.

I grunted, clearing my throat as I tried to find a witty and manly answer to that when a shadow moved down the street and I had to push Ophelia back and out of sight of the two people laying on the ground. We leave them there, many more pressing issues to handle.

Tall and hunched he walked down the street, bathed in the shadows with the air of *Jack The Eater*, surrounding him and I knew it was show time.

CHAPTER
SIXTEEN

Ophelia
One Hell of a Team - AmaLee

"We make one Hell of a team, Soul Raiser," Blake whispered into my ear as he wrapped an arm around me and kept us concealed within the shadows. My breathing was heavy and sensual. A small tendril of the mood moments ago still twirled around me in a gentle caress that had my heart dipping and my skin pebbled. "Where did you learn to fight like that?"

"I'm an author, Blake. Every single one of my heroines is deadly and lethal. They know how to fight, so naturally, I do too. I am my work. Why do you think I was in the grave-yard tonight? I become my characters so I can write them to justice." I breathlessly replied, my throat a little raspy.

"Huh," he uttered and I smirked at having had a way to befuddle him.

It was endearing, actually. Watching him all flustered. I

reached behind me and palmed his cock, which shriveled more than a shrimp trying to keep its shell.

"Aw, baby. You were right. I do love your cock."

He jittered away from me and I chuckled so hard that he had to clamp a hand over my mouth.

All I needed now was the other around my throat. Just as I thought it, he obliged and I shuddered in stimulation. "Don't play with me, sweetheart," he growled with a dangerous lilt to his tone and I purred into his palm. When he pulled away, I looked up at him over my shoulder and whispered back, "Why? When I so enjoy your punishments."

His eyes narrowed and widened at the same time, thick lips puckered as he nodded his head in amusement. "Careful, love. The wicked in you is starting to show."

"Oh, but isn't that how you want me?" I teased. The sexual tension between us burned hotter than a volcano. I struggled to keep my hands to myself, the need to run them over every dip and curve of his defined muscles a compulsion. He awoke something inside of me that was hard to explain. Something primal and raw that was pure desire and absolutely nothing else. When he surrounded me, quietness fell and my mind finally calmed. My fuel was his energy, and everything he led me into I went into willingly, sedated by his intoxication.

The fact we were now stalking a dude that ate flesh, was a distant ick in the back of my mind. The night was at its darkest, right before the creeping hours of dawn that would soon encroach on us. Murky fog snaked along the ground, coiling higher and higher. When I peeked back out from the cave of our darkness, I saw a tall figure stalking down the street. He was humming, dressed in a long black trench coat that dragged along the ground behind him, and a top hat that honestly made him look like he belonged in a different era. The sound of his warped tune rang through the air and sent a shiver down my spine. Because who the fuck hums before they eat somebody's ass?

Blake.

That was who.

"Do you know what he's going to do next?" I whispered, unable to tear my eyes away from the shadow that moved closer toward us.

"Yes," he whispered back. "Do you trust me?" he asked for the hundredth time tonight and each time I answered yes, he threw me into even deeper waters. There was a lilt of humor to his tone and it had me craning my neck back to glare at him in suspicion.

"No, not when you say it like that," I retorted. The sound of his voice was mockingly sinister. Like he had some twisted game up his leather sleeve and I had this daunting feeling that I'd be the butt of that joke.

"Remember, love. Make it believable." He chuckled before he let me go abruptly and shoved me, sending me staggering into the street.

Shit.

I spun in a circle, needing to see how far this creepy bastard was from where I stood, only to squeal and jump back when his nose was practically touching mine. The lanky six-foot-seven sicko was hunched over, bent lower to my height, and just as I was about to scream the freak sniffed me and all I could do in response to that was draw my head back onto my shoulders in disbelief. He groaned and rotated his head like it was on a swivel stick. Then he licked the air, did a little happy dance and spun in a maniacal circle of his own, waving his hands in the air like a demented clown doing a party trick.

"Ooo, trick, trick because I just found myself a delicious treat!"

Fuck no.

"Listen freak!"

"No, no! Meals do not speak. Hush now, we'll have you in the pot soon enough," he chastised and my brows hit my hairline at the balls of this human-flesh-eating dick face.

Had he ever...

Nope. No. Not tonight, Satan.

"We?" I questioned as I took a tentative step backward and scanned the street around me expecting to see somebody else jumping from the dead of night. Trust Blake not to give me the heads up that I'd be fighting a cackle of freaks.

"The cheek!" he exclaimed in heated protest.

"The nose!" he squealed in sour retort.

"The lips!"

"The tit!"

Then the Jekyll and Hyde bit stopped and he stood there eerily still staring at nothing as he seemed to think over whatever the fuck he was just arguing with himself about. "Hmm, the tit. I could eat a tit tonight."

My head snapped toward the corner I was standing five seconds ago with Blake and saw him leaning up against the brick so casually, leg hiked up like he was moments before he spun me into a dance that still had my mind hazy and kicked the ass of a pervert. The demented fucker was laughing at me. I narrowed my eyes, ready to just knock this freaky dude out so we could get on with the killing part of my wild All Hallows' Eve adventures, but when I turned back to him, the dude lurched a hand into my hair and began dragging me along the street kicking and screaming.

"Get the fuck off me!" I bellowed, digging in my heels

and scratching at the hidden wrists of his flesh that was lost behind the fabric of his trench coat. "Let me go!" Through everything that had happened tonight, through all of the sick things that I had watched happen, this was the thing that terrified me the most.

Being powerless.

Nothing I did gave me purchase. None of my fancy self-defense moves could work when I was a long, lone, and limp spaghetti noodle flailing in the wind. He dragged me with unnatural ease, and my heart beat a frantic rhythm into my ribcage. My entire chest ached brutally, the pain feathering down into my ribs and taking root in my stomach.

Bile burned in the back of my throat and each time it rose higher, ready to spew from me, I feared that I would drop dead when the next breath came so belatedly because of it.

Just when I found my footing, I managed to twist in his hold and pull back, he yanked a fistful of my hair and held it in his unwavered grip.

Fuck it.

I could live with being bald. I couldn't live with being dead.

When I worked my way to standing in front of him and righted myself, batting the downfall of my hair from my face and tried to catch a breath, he laughed and shoved me in the chest. Confusion had my eyes wide, then I went flying backward, it wasn't pavement that greeted me though. It was a covering of darkness and a metal thud as I hit my head on something that echoed back at me with a ding.

As I blinked open my dazed eyes, I noticed I'd been tossed into the back of a van, and the engine that purred to life, vibrating underneath me, instilled fear into my horrified heart.

I kicked my feet and scurried to my knees. The jerk in the vehicle had me flying forward and as I landed with my chest flat against the ground, I turned my head at the last second to prevent myself from busting my nose. I stilled when a glass door in a small refrigerator hummed beside me.

A decapitated head with a missing eye stared back at me.

I gasped and rolled to my back immediately. I froze as I stared at the ceiling almost as if I could pretend that I never saw such a thing and that that *thing* sure as fuck never saw me, "Blake!" I shrilled wildly. "I'm going to kill you!"

"I'm already dead, sweetheart!" his voice whispered around me with a taunt that had me slamming my fists against the side of the van and screaming bloody murder.

CHAPTER
SEVENTEEN

Blake

Follow Me Down - The Pretty Reckless

I lingered within the shadows, too hyped up on Ophelia's screams and insults to intervene just yet. She's strapped naked to the table. Once he brought her back to his slaughterhouse, he tossed her into a cell and told her to strip. The fact he hadn't touched her yet was the only reason I was playing this out.

She craved the excitement and more than anything, she craved the power.

I just watched that be stolen from her, so I know that our next kill will be fucking glorious. I wanted more from her than dishing out a few striking kicks and punches.

I had her exactly where I wanted her most.

Utterly and dependently dependent on my mercy.

After she told him to go and eat himself—which seemed like the biggest insult possible—he flipped a switch on the wall and the cell floors began to heat under her feet.

He had told her to strip or fry so naturally with a slur of the most degrading insults known to mankind, she stripped, then threw her clothes in his face.

I chuckled, shaking my head at the frustration etched into the features of her pretty face.

"Blake, you asshole! If you can still fuck with that dick of yours, I can still cut it off!" she vowed in a furied bellow and I flinched, covering my cock from those scorching words.

What was it with this chick and cutting off dicks?

I winced and looked over my shoulder. As I did a double take, bile rose in the back of my throat. A row of mutilated cocks swam in some jars of vile-looking liquid, side by side on the shelving unit that held other body parts. Hearts, livers, and for some fucked up reason, vaginas, that were completely intact. I shuddered, dreading to think why the fuck he would keep them if he claimed in his article he couldn't eat them.

"Freak," I uttered under my breath as I shivered in disgust.

Ophelia thrashed in her restraints. Thick black straps crossed her ample tits, pelvis, and forehead. The metal table rattled and I rolled my eyes. She'd break a bone if she carried on.

But that was my woman.

A fighter.

Fuck, I thrived on that about her.

The sight of her milky flesh was enough to bring my cock back to life, I had to readjust it in my jeans. The hardness of it was a pain that tented against the denim as it chafed.

Little witch.

"Seriously, Blake. This is not funny!" she screamed and I blew out a heavy breath.

Guess it was time to free her before she went and had an aneurysm before I could finish having my wicked fun with her. The best thing about her was that even though her fear was evident, she held a stronger irritation.

Defiance.

She wouldn't let this mad man see her fear. She wouldn't give him what he wanted most. She'd sooner die than fall prey any more than she had.

That was what got under her skin the most though.

Being prey at all.

And the injustice.

Cute.

Just as I stepped from the shadows Barry The Funky came back into the room knocking a steel tray as he passed. With a huge bottle of something clear in his hands, he placed it on the table beside Ophelia before he flicked off the cap and lifted it again.

"Get the fuck away from me you sick, twisted mother-fucking fuck cunt!" she seethed with venom. I could almost feel the poison in her words lick against me as she spat them into the air around us.

"Hmm, hmmm, hmmm. Food, food, food," I baulked when he started singing in such a low and drawn-out tone that he sounded like a sea creature luring sailors to their death.

"No, no! Fucking no!" she screamed as he dumped half a gallon of that clear liquid onto her flesh and then reached behind him to pick up large vials of seasoning that he sprinkled all over her.

I was too struck dumb to react as quickly as I intended and before I could blink, those insidious, vile little hands were all over my woman. Kneading the oil and seasoning into her skin with skilled fingers that were familiar with massaging their meat before butchering it.

Fuck no, Barry The Cannibal needed to die.

I was sure that Ophelia was watching me, but when my furious eyes flickered back toward her, to let her know I was coming, her eyes were trained to the ceiling. Her entire body was slack as she moaned in sultry sensation, "Oh, yeah. Skinner. That's the spot." When the man stilled, confusion furrowing his brows, she tutted, "No, no. Carry on now, that's just where I needed you most."

Cheeky little...

I once said anger wasn't an emotion I was all too familiar with.

I lied.

Fury consumed me like a wildfire destroying an expanse of a miles-long forest and just as easily *and* as quickly as the foliage in those forests combusted, I went up in the flames of my rage.

I stalked from the shadows, switchblade in hand. As I stabbed it into the man's shoulder and snarled, he bellowed a roar of pain. I drew the blade across the back of his neck and created small and painful wounds that would have burned just as soon as I ripped him away from her by my grip on the back of his neck. All of the clutter he had around us toppled over in my temper, I wasn't clean or maintained when I thrashed him about like a fish out of water dying for the first drops of rain. I slashed and carved, gutting him everywhere my blade could reach in my unorganized attack and he sloppily struggled to defend himself.

"Don't *ever*!" I hissed, unable to keep my furious tone even. "Touch what is mine." When I spun, I saw the huge pot that was boiling in the corner. It was larger than an industrial pot and I turned my lips up in violation knowing what he was about to have used it for. I charged forward, the bubbled popping and hiss of the shimmering flow was sweet music to my ears while I shoved his head into it.

The water gurgled, sloshing around his head as he screamed into the heat that was peeling the flesh from his bones with such harrowing anguish that I would have felt a pang of something humane had he not just had his vile hands on my woman. One of my hands held his head in the pot, my skin was hidden under the chaos and as cold as ever. The other reached for the meat cleaver that hung above our head with other types of butchering knives and I yanked it from the hook to bring it thundering down on his right wrist, removing one of his hands before I moved on to the other.

By the time I got to the second hand, he was still, no longer fighting as he fell unmovable in the boiling water. I drew my blade across his throat for good measure, wanting to make sure he was dead before I turned around and prowled back toward Ophelia with vengeful wrath in my dark complexities. "Now, love... I am sure I misheard you, because there was *no* way my good girl encouraged another man to touch her, *right?*" I asked slowly as my eyes stalked her heaving chest wanting to see what was hidden beneath it.

"Now, love... I'm sure I misunderstood the situation because there was *no* way *my* man threw me to a cannibal to become a delectable snack of his, *right?*" she retorted with an arrogant look on her face and I sneered as I loomed over her.

"Such dangerous games you play, sweetheart."

"Yeah, yeah. I'm ready for my punishment now." She smirked and I narrowed my eyes at her. She never seemed to not amaze me. Never seemed to not drive me rabid with a need so intoxicating that it burned hot like coals in my core. A parasite that fed from my bones. She was ingrained, carved, and etched into the very fibers of my dead being and I had no way to purge her from my system. "Would you really have let him eat me?" she asked, all sense of deflective humor gone.

"The thought of another man touching you drove me to cut off those very same hands that did... What do you think, love?"

Insecurity bled into her gaze and I smirked, knowing the perfect way to erase it. The steel blade glistened under the low and dim lights in the dungeon-like home we resided within. I placed the tip just above the thick strap that curved around her pelvic bone and she heaved a deep breath, holding the sharp and cold-sounding intake hostage within her lungs. Slowly, ever so fucking slowly I dragged that cool steel blade up her core, over her belly button, and just below the point of her sternum.

It was a smooth caress, one I'd designed to leave her guessing, right up until the moment I slipped it under the strap holding down her chest and cut it free, allowing her ample breasts to spill out from under the support and expose them to my dark and hungry eyes. "The only one who gets to eat these fine tits, sugar, is *me*," I mused right before I descended like a vulture from the sky devouring its prey. I took her puckered bud into my mouth and teased her with the swirl of my tongue.

She gasped, all of that air she had held deep within her chest burst from her with a heated gust of arousal that had her moaning loudly. She writhed as much as she could, which wasn't a lot considering her bottom half was restrained to the table. As I played with one sweet-tasting nipple, I pinched the other one and she hissed.

"Fuck! Oh, God!" she purred.

I stopped. Pulled back and looked her dead in the eye. "Do I look like a saint, darling?" I asked with dangerous, narrowed eyes. "Because I'd definitely class this as a sin."

"Say it," I ordered. "Say I'm your Devil."

"You're my Devil!" she cried, her thighs trembled as she quivered. "Blake, I can't, not with my breasts. It drives me insane, it goes straight to my clit and I feel like I'll explode if I don't come. Please! Please, help me!"

How fucking beautiful she sounded when she begged with those thick and desirable lips of hers. The lips so sensually parted and opened for me.

My cock ached, was heavy, and pulsated under the need to drive into her wet cunt. I freed myself, allowing it to spring largely up against my core, then shook when the cool air kissed against my heated head of arousal. "You do such depraved and naughty things to my body, Soul Raiser. The body that hasn't been alive in so many years. Why should I give you a reprieve when I can't escape this sensation you've planted within me?" I moved around the table to stand by her head, the tip of my cock siding along the seams of her thick lips.

"Please!" she begged. "It's started and I can't stop it!"

"Can't stop what, love?" I asked as I rocked and she opened her mouth to chase me.

"The need to come for you!"

"Ah, such a dilemma," I mused as her frantic eyes followed mine as I descended again slowly to her heavy left breast, thrusting my cock fully into the back of her throat. "But I'm ravenous, babe. I guess you'll just have to wait." I took her perfect, rose-tipped nipple back into my mouth and trailed my blade back down her center, in the same taunting caress that had tears trailing down her cheeks. She gasped and choked, the struggle to adjust to my size and abrupt intrusion difficult.

But she did it and she did it fucking gloriously with an enthusiasm that had my balls drawn up tight.

There were no tears sweeter than the tears of pleasure.

When the blade stopped on top of the strap around the curve of her thighs, I continued until I could slip the knife under it. She moved her head to the side as I drew my hips backward and slipped free from her perfected mouth. "Blake!"

"That's my name, love," I whispered against her when I pulled back from her breast too, knowing my cool breath would torment her. "Oh, how wonderfully you beg for me. Tell me, Ophelia. Tell me how much you need it. How much you need *me*." I flipped my knife, bringing the end of the handle to her weeping cunt, moving around the table so I had a better angle. I had to tighten my grip as it slipped through her heat easily with the slickness of her arousal. She moaned and it sounded feral, like the receptors of her brain were telling her that she was seduced and turned her into a savage that would fight for the high she craved the most.

"I need it! I need it, Blake, I need you! Please, oh Satan, please!" she wept, and I smirked. As I ran my thumb along the curve of her cheek, I gathered the tears at the exact same time I thrust the handle of the knife into her ready, wanton, and greedy cunt. "Oh, yes!" Her back arched as her pussy clenched. Her thighs trembled, the invasion tight as her legs were forced together.

"So fucking gorgeous, love," I rasped as I withdrew the

knife and thrust the end into her mouth as I sucked my thumb into mine.

Together, we both moaned and it was intoxicating.

"Taste yourself, sugar. Taste how fucking delectable you taste to me when I'm devouring nectar as addictive as yours." I hummed, the vibration feathering down my flexed thumb. "These tears of lust? Just as addicting."

Then I moved to the foot of the table and cut the straps. She sighed in relief and then gasped when I used the shredded fabric to tie her ankles to each leg of the steel table, spread eagle. My deft finger circled her clit, a sensual caress that had a mewl whispering from the back of her throat. Her head thrashed side to side and her knees bent and buckled as they tried to close and hold me where she needed me most.

I was entranced, my gaze entirely focused on her slick core and her captivating pussy. I was bewitched, unable to look away from her succulent pink folds that glistened and bloomed like the petals on a rose, exposing to me her ravishing cunt. I inserted the handle of the knife once again into her soaked core and started to fuck her slowly, experimentally. Enraptured by watching the way it moved in and out of her so perfectly. I stood fascinated as she panted and purred, crying out from the pleasure I was bestowing upon her.

"*So*, fucking wet for me," I noted with appreciation that had her whimpering at my praise. "*So*, fucking good for me."

"Blake!"

"Just one more moment, love. I want to remember this," I whispered as I slowly bent at the waist to embed my face between her thighs. As the tender seconds passed, I moved my face closer, watching the knife intensely before I wrapped my cool mouth around her clit and sucked on her even more slowly than could be considered a tease.

It was more like a starving man eating the crumbs of his last slice of cake, savoring every bit with the intent to make it last forever.

I could feel the handle as it glided swiftly inside of her and strongly against my chin.

"Blake!" she roared, the steel table shaking as she writhed from my remarkable ability to take her to the cliff and dangle her from the edge of it without ever letting go.

"You brought me back from the dead, Soul Raiser. Let me enjoy this," I hummed against her and she whimpered, flexing her lips and firmly pushing her core into me so her cunt was riding my face with the pressure she needed the most.

I lost my shit, all of my control withered and died, turning to ash that drifted around us as I consumed her. I picked up the pace and fucked her savagely with the handle as I feasted on her clit like a man possessed.

And I was...

Possessed.

Possessed with the need to taste her release as it slid down the back of my throat, dripping from my chin.

"No more games, Ophelia. Come. Come for me!" I demanded in a vicious snarl that told her I was close to my end.

Like the good girl that she was, she never kept me waiting. She exploded, gushing into my mouth as I sneered like a barbaric man with no control left at all. I swallowed her release and thrived for more as I pulled back, climbed her body, and thrust my cock deep into her core. Fully seated, I moaned into her ear, the pleasure too much of a burden to bear.

But suffer I would because no matter how torturous this was, she was still the best thing I'd ever felt. I wrapped my hand around her throat and unlike all the other times, *this* time I wanted her to see the abyss she dragged me from. She spluttered and choked as I flexed my hips and drove into her as I ventured beyond the hilt, wanting to be as deep inside of her as I could possibly go. She spluttered and choked, her eyes rolled back in her head and I grunted and groaned, so close to my end as I rutted into her with a wild and untamed abandon that made the table squeal beneath us.

"Come, Ophelia," I demanded harshly. Desperately. "I want you to come for me again, love. Right. The Fuck. *Now*," I gritted between clenched teeth, then snapped my tightly shut eyes open to watch the details of her face contort into a frantic and unbridled type of pleasure as I pinched her clit and together, we came undone in an explosion that was cosmic.

The entity of the galaxies fell down upon us as we danced amongst the stars.

"Holy fucking shit, Soul Raiser," I breathed as I fell slack on top of her quivering form. "I'll never tire of you."

As I let go of her throat, her groggy eyes flutter open slowly as she rasped, "I should allow another man's hands on me more often for a sweet fuck like that, baby."

The fuck she say to me?

With a snarl, I cut the rest of her restraints and flipped her to her knees. As I climbed off the table, I yanked, bringing her with me. As her feet hit the ground, my hand in between her shoulder blades, I pushed her to fold over the table again and drove myself into her tight, tender, and raw cunt from behind. I fisted her hair, pulled her head back, and blew a cool breath along the column of her throat.

"Then, darling. I think I need to remind you why the fuck you're *mine*."

"Make Hate To Me" by Citizen Soldier bellowed around us and fuck me if that song wasn't the mood for our next ball-achingly good fuck.

CHAPTER
EIGHTEEN

Ophelia
Bring Me to Life - Evanescence

Sweat glistened on my skin, my chest heaved as I fought for my every breath with increasing difficulty. Sensual flutters still caressed my skin. I craved more, my body ached but my soul protested, still in shock from being drawn from my body as I danced above it at the hands of a fuck that was out of this world.

Despite the rawness of it, I had never felt more appreciated and desired. More taken care of like a delicate flower tenderly held even with the prospect of it harboring poisonous petals.

When I was around him, I never knew if I was the cure or the disease. He made me want to be so bad, even after I spent my whole life being moderately good.

Blake was a special kind of man. A man that pushed me to my limits and never failed to bring me back from the edge with wanting more.

With *begging* for more.

He stole my essence and infused it with his own. I was obsessed and I knew that at this very moment in time I would do anything that he asked of me.

I would *become* all that he needed me to be.

Because he was now my everything.

The air I needed to breathe.

I would never let go of him or the things he has taught me. I've become dependent on the rush, on the adrenaline that coursed through my veins. When he looked at me, I felt like the only person in the world that mattered. That if the world was to burn to ash, he would stand amidst the flames still staring at me with those intense, soul-deep eyes. It was out of this world, something no words could ever even touch. The constellations danced in my vision and after a moment, they all began to look like him.

The dead man who saved me from a boring and tedious life of rules and morals.

Bloody mutilation and orgasmic desire are a lethal concoction and I've been contaminated with its hazardous smoke.

I ran my hands through his damp hair, riddled with the sweat of our combined heat and I moaned, the feel of him against me sensational. "Thank you," I whispered. "Thank you for tonight."

"I thought the taste of you would be better than killing you," he murmured and I could hear the smirk in his tone. "I'm glad that I was right."

"Hmm, hmm," I hummed.

"The night isn't over yet, love. Close, but not quite."

"What? Blake, how many more people can we kill?" I asked sleepily, spent from the night's activities and fading fast into a deep sleep.

"Just one, sweetheart. A special one."

He had me intrigued, but I was too tired to protest or ask any more questions. He moved to my side and pulled me into his arms as we crawled back onto the steel table. The number of people who had probably been slaughtered on this very table, was not even a vile thought in my mind when I cuddled closer to him and laid my head on his chest as I stroked my hands over his smooth skin. The effortless feel of his perfect core acted like a black silken hypnotism that had me drifting a sea of dreamily content. "Blake."

"I know, sugar. Sleep now, I'll protect you from every dead thing, *other* than *me*."

I smiled against his cool skin and did exactly that, falling into a deep sleep.

When I woke up, I was cradled into the crook of his arm, his dark eyes stared down at me as he smoothed the hair back from my face so he could caress my cheek. "The more I watch you, the more beautiful you become."

I clear my throat softly and smile up at him, "I never knew a serial killer could be so sweet."

"Then you've never met the right serial killer." He winked before he shifted to sit up and pulled me with him. I threw my leg over his waist and sat on his lap as his large hands stroked over the expanse of my back. "You ready to finish the night, love? Dawn is close."

I nodded, then narrowed my eyes, "You keep talking like you're going to leave."

He frowned, then looked away. "I might have to. I'm not sure how long you summoned me here for."

I never thought of that and it stabbed fear into my heart. Fear encased with a deeply penetrating sorrow that I might lose this. I opened my mouth to say just that when he placed a finger against my parted lips. "No, sweetheart. Let's not think about it. Let's just enjoy our next kill."

I fluttered my eyes, batting away the tears that pooled within them. I wouldn't cry and I wouldn't lose him. I summoned him once, I'd summon him again if I had to.

Because this serial killer was mine.

And even though I was sure of all of that, I still couldn't crawl from his lap without uttering the words that have crept into my heart and held it in a vise ever since.

I held him closer, my hands curled within the thick strands of his hair, a desperation to never let him go, a demon clawing at my insides. I felt that if he withered away and faded from my hold, I'd fade with him. "I think I've fallen in love with you," I whispered, my eyes on his as I hoped he could see the devotion there. I couldn't shy away from this, I couldn't hide away from the fact that this was my heart sitting on the end of my sleeve. I had to tell him, I needed him to know.

I felt like I always would.

"Good, because I think I fell in love with you the moment you tried to drown me in holy water," he husked in a deep honey-coated tone. I expected him to smile at me with that brooding, dangerously lethal smile of his, but instead, he stared back at me with such seriousness, that my heart skipped a beat and a breath caught in the back of my throat.

The devil take me, I never wanted that look to disappear.

"Okay," I whispered, then he finally smirked at me with amusement in those dark eyes. "Okay, one last kill."

"Just the words I love to hear coming out of the mouth of my woman. So damn sexy, love." He smirked as he yanked me in closer and I yelped before I laughed at the exciting energy behind it. "Let's go then." As he did that ghostly shit again, I never felt as sick as I did the first time and I smirked at the thought I could get used to the craziness.

We ended up on a residential street. My clothing stitched back to my body and I assumed he did that when he teleported us here. He never seemed to stop surprising me and that was one of the things that had me hook, line and sinker. I was a goner the first moment he ever touched me and every cold moment he had touched me ever since.

The street was in darkness, every suburban home shrouded in an abyss that we could hardly see pass under the low lighting of the street lamps. He took my hand and together we stalked down the sidewalk like reapers of the night. Following his lead, I watched each house and searched for any kind of movement.

I listened for any kind of sound.

There.

It was a whispering sob that was making its way through the silence. The soft sound of a quiet cry for help drifted from a person who tried to conceal the devastation with a pillow. Her soul was crying for a hand to help her, but her mortal mouth kept her from screaming out and capturing the help of those who surrounded her, those who could *actually* help her.

I turned to Blake, confusion creased the lines of my face, and had my eyes hooded with furrowed brows. "What's that?" I asked quietly.

He turned us, wrapped his hands around my waist, and pulled me back into his cool chest. He settled his chin onto my shoulder and whispered, "Inside that house is a mother and a disabled child. The mother abuses her. Uses half of the medication to sedate her daughter and the other half for herself. She isolated the girl. In the quiet moments of the night, that's the only time she's free to scream." A chill skated down my spine, and I shivered at his words. "She knows if she cries too loudly, if her mother knew there were moments of reprieve, it would be worse. That she would kill her. During the night, it's the only time she can be free from the walls of her mind. She keeps herself quiet because she has lost all hope that anybody would be able to save her."

I was horrified, enraged even. I had just had my power stolen from me. Strapped down to a table by a madman that wanted to eat me. I was weak, helpless, and needed saving. Blake saved me, even though it was his damn fault that I was there in the first place. This whole night has been showing me what it means to walk on the other side of darkness. To be a vigilante doing deplorable things to another human being and in turn saving countless others.

Everyone that we killed tonight deserved it.

There was no justice behind the iron bars of a cell.

They would still get to see the rising of another sun.

It didn't matter that they may have moments of misery, somebody alive and able to laugh at another joke, even one told by another inmate, was too much of an injustice to sit right with me.

Justice? It was in the slashing of a blade wielded by an even worse man who put those evil talents to good use.

Now, I was faced with more than just watching and learning.

Observing what it meant for another human being to commit such vicious acts to another living soul.

Now I was pissed and I didn't know what to do with that manic feeling that brewed inside of me.

Blake tightened his hold of me in his arms, and we were in the hallway of a quiet suburban home a second later. Quiet except for those small sobs I could still hear ringing in my ears like the echo of a war drum leading me into battle.

"Blake," I breathed.

"Yes, Soul Raiser?"

"Make it fucking hurt. Nobody who does this to an innocent child should be allowed to know what a peaceful death feels like." The unfeeling tone in my voice would have startled me if I wasn't already lost to the violence and bloodshed of tonight.

"Uh-ah, love," he rasped back and my back straightened as I turned to look up at him from over my shoulder. "This one is all yours, sugar."

For a moment, all I could do was stare at him.

A war waged within my mind.

Then, a short second later and lighter with less of the weight that came with the burden of great turmoil and conflict, I stepped into the mother's bedroom with a feral grin on my face.

CHAPTER
NINETEEN

Bonnie
Killer in the Mirror - Set It Off

The night is supposed to conceal our demons, keeping them hidden from the pure minds that would hang us for the morality that dwelt in their darkened hearts.

It's the one place where you would find your monsters lingering in the ominous shadows.

That was what we were told.

Every day of our lives, the things soaked in crimson were the things we should be wary of. That the ugly and the depraved were the sins we should burn with holy water, and every malicious thought should be purged from our minds and souls with an iron cross.

But when you play it right, the night was also the void that let our personal demons out to play with nobody to bear witness to such an incredible dark art of wickedness. Society couldn't condemn you for the sins cloaked in the veil of a lethal abyss.

We had been taught to think anything unholy was wrong.

But that was a lie and anybody still accustomed to such warped ways had my pity.

We all held it within us. That was nothing to be ashamed of.

A parasite that was waiting for the right time to consume your withering bones and instilled you with the strength of a monster fit to rid this world of all its evils.

The *night*?

Had always been my favorite thing, no matter what side of it I got.

Blood ran in rivers down my arms, and crimson plasma splattered against my lips.

I stared back at the wall, seeing stars in the mayhem, and smirked to myself.

Why was blood so pretty?

Hmmm.

I ran my toes along the silken ground and smeared the essence that surrounded me as I went. Humming the theme song to *Stranger Things*, I licked my fingers clean before I kicked the body at my feet. Then like a demon possessed, I threw myself onto the corpse and rained down maddening punches, licking the air that seemed to become electrified in my psychotic state. Everything tasted sweet and glorious, but I *needed* more. I let out a throaty sneer, putting *Scary Movie* and their what's uppp scene to shame as I lost myself to the rejuvenating euphoria that came with bloodshed at utter carnage.

Nobody talked about what a beautiful thing death was.

How final and complete.

Could a human brain even comprehend the magnitude of such a thing?

How we were here, until we weren't.

Until the lights went out and then we were where?

Nowhere and everywhere?

Well, I got a secret for you, sugar.

There was nothing after death. Nothing but torment from the thing that killed you.

Like so many others, that asshole's happily never ever would feature my twisted mug and my sexy as fuck sinister smirk.

As I carved the heart from her chest, I held it in my hand. Her pale face stunning under the light of the moon, breaking through the cracks. With eyes as dark as chocolate glossed over in a yellow sheen of crystalized balls, she stared back at me. It didn't feel like I thought it would.

Killing someone.

The heart was hard, encased with squiggly edges—with curves and crevices that hid away all of the little valves that once kept this useless thing beating.

Now I was eye to eye with it, holding it before my very face with a steady hand placed over my own heart. I just couldn't seem to feel the connection.

The horror.

The fear.

Which I presumed a normal person would. All I held though was unbridled curiosity that coursed through my veins like burning embers of a great fire. I needed to know more. I needed to breach the barrier of inquisitiveness that kept me up at night. I needed to make some kind of sense of how I was alive, with a heart that beat under my palm and that was the only difference between me and the dead bitch beneath me. I never used to be like this. Killing with a gun was always so much easier. But now, getting up close and personal with the bodies that stain my hands red, has a smirk on my lips and my mind running wild with the possibilities of what else I could find when cutting a bitch.

Anyway.

Enough about me.

Welcome to the slaughterhouse, the place born of bloody desires and a curiosity that would most definitely kill the cat.

Happy Halloween!

CHAPTER
TWENTY

Clyde

Hit Me With Your Best Shot - Pat Benatar

I t was an exquisite thing, watching the love of my life covered in the blood of her victims. Tonight, she really let go. She gave it all her wicked best, and I could not have been prouder of the game we played. Though sick and twisted, this game of *dead, dead, fucker* really got my dick hard.

Tonight, she took her role and made it her bitch. Through every kill, she really made me believe in this psycho game we played.

I really believed she was innocent right up until the moment she let go and slaughtered the bitch who hurt her child.

You see, we were both dead.

Gunned down in our prime, oh so many years ago.

The injustice, *damn* that bitch stung.

Then, we upped our game. The only gang we needed was one of two. Just me and my Bonnie. The need for violence only grew and we built a good gig from the afterlife.

This?

Tonight?

Well, this was all just our foreplay, baby.

Every year, on All Hallows' Eve, we rise upon the witching hour.

We came back to earth and we slaughtered like a couple in love should and every damn year, we pretended to be somebody we were not.

This year, Bon picked the sweet little author all ripe and ready for the big bad serial killer to come and corrupt her. The woman she played? Was alive and out there somewhere, writing all of her research down in some novel. We pottered around her house earlier tonight, but of course, she couldn't see us.

Because we never wanted her to.

Did you notice that part?

All of the little breadcrumbs we left you on our sick adventure.

There was a reason confusion was the first thing Dale felt and not horror.

Me?

Well, I played the man called Blake. Dug the name. But the case and the cop? That was all real. The serial killer paid us a pretty penny in Hell's fire to avenge his murder back down in Hell, so we did.

Getting to be anybody we choose to be, and at the end of the night, still returned back to each other's arms, *oh*... I just shuddered. It was a beautiful thing of utter carnage.

We walked through the graveyard, my bare toes sunk into the soil as I held her delicate hand in mine, "Well, love?

Does this year outshine all of the others?" I asked as I turned my gaze to her stunning features.

"Oh, Clyde. This year is definitely one of the best, it was so sexy how you were all domineering and passionate. I can't remember the last time I came so hard, I could feel actual life coursing back through me. It sure was a feeling to thrive on," she replied with a wicked smirk and a sexy as the devil's mistress southern accent.

I growled as I pulled her into my arms.

"Any ideas who you want to be next year, darling?" I questioned as I tucked a loose strand of her hair behind her ear, then caressed her smooth cheek.

"Hmm," she hummed as she thought it over. "Well that depends on who my kill will be, doesn't it? You know, I've never understood why any of the others never want to come back to earth on Halloween."

"They enjoy it too much in Hell, they don't have to feel anything other than content. Human emotion, it's icky, and once you die and that shit fades away, why the hell would you want to live through it again? Lucky for us, it never makes our return boring." I chuckled, as I placed a tender kiss on her thick lips.

Together, hand in hand, we walked under the willow tree and back into the grave.

"Until next year, love."

EPILOGUE

Bonnie

Crazy Bitch - Buckcherry

"Is he dead? Is my rapist dead?" Kelsie asked as she smacked her lips and the annoying clap of her gum flittered around me.

I cringed, cranking my neck as the feeling of irritation at the sound washed over me.

"What about my mother? Did you kill her?" Aime shouted over Kelsie with a bratty attitude that had me rolling my eyes. In the afterlife, her disabilities were gone. She stood before me in shit kicker Doc Martins, cut-off boy shorts and a crop top that showed a little too much flesh. By the time her mother killed her, she had just reached sixteen.

Why was she in Hell?

Because the fun fact is, we get to choose.

There was no heaven, given the fact that God was a figment of the human imagination created to help them find the strength not to fear the Devil that lurks beneath their feet. Like a holy savior, you'd tell your kids about at bedtime, to stop them screaming that the boogeyman was going to jump out if the closet and eat them.

Truth was, there was only the veil between worlds called the cosmic plane, or you have down here.

Hell.

Burning in shit loads of fun.

In the cosmic plane, you were basically still on earth, moping around like some deranged and lonely fool, where nobody could see you and interaction was impossible. You became a ghost or some other kind of freaky shit if you became powerful enough like a poltergeist.

I killed her mother at her request and her sweet payment was hellfire, in the exact same way she had dreamed of killing her for all of those years she was under the hand of her torture. So I guess you could add impure thoughts to the list if you really needed a reason that made sense to the simplicity of a human mind.

"What about Dale? Is that fucker dead? I hope you skinned him exactly how I asked!" Robbie grunted, a sick excitement bright in his usually dull serial killer eyes.

"Not exactly," Clyde answered. "He looked at my woman so I had to improvise."

"What?" He scoffed in outrage. "That was not the fucking deal, man." He stepped toward Clyde and lifted his arm, fist clenched and just as he swung, I was there, shattering his bones as they crumbled in my palm. He hissed, a small cry of pain leaving him as I shoved him away from me as he pulled his broken hand into a cradle against his chest.

"If you wanted it done right, you should have gone up top yourself, asshole," I stated in a bored tone, daring him to come at me next.

He widened his eyes and recoiled in disgust. "Fuck no.

Hell is much more fun, why the two of you like going up there so much is fucking insane. All those burdens? All the heavy shit? The turmoil and human emotion? No, fuck that. Down here, it's simple. There is no anguish just a lot of pussy and some fun, fucking, fun!" He smirked as he danced his shoulders and flexed his hips.

"Then shut the fuck up." I smirked and he smirked back with a wink of conceit in his eyes.

"Seriously, though. Are they all dead? Did you kill the cannibal? That fucking prick actually had the nerve to say my pussy was too chewy. Like what the fuck? He degrades and mutilates me and *then* complains my cunt isn't tender enough? *He's* the fucking cunt, I'll tell you that much," Alex rampaged as she folded her arms across her slight chest.

Robbie looked at her, a wicked gleam in his eyes. "Well, babe. I can definitely say that pussy tastes just right." She punched him in the arm and he chuckled like a dumb jock even though he was far from it.

"You paid, we provided and we sure as fuck had fun doing it. Everyone has been murdered as per your request and hand-delivered to the Devil himself. You can go watch their torture once they go through processing.

Another fun fact?

Hell was also kinda like a prison for the bad folk up on earth.

All those bastards we killed? They get sent to Devil's County. Satan's best demons will then book 'em, process them, toss them into their respective cells, then open their screens to the audience who are able to watch their execution.

Over.

And.

Over.

Again.

For all of eternity. Sweet fucking bliss.

We could also buy those souls for the right price and enslave them.

Lockie was good to us like that.

Aime jumped in place as she clapped her hands. "Fuck yes. I've been saving for this. That cunt-bitch is mine!"

Then we all dispersed and I kissed Clyde with a passion that defied the very flames of Hell and moved toward the dance floor after our welcome home.

"Crazy Bitch" by Buckcherry echoed around the pit in central Hell. I danced, moving my hips to the bass that echoed around me, smacking my lips as I chewed on a piece of gum and picked my nails with the end of my blade.

It wasn't as annoying when *I* did it.

Souls who chose the fires of Hell partied, writhing against one another in a concoction of wild desire and unbridled lust with a shit ton of manic energy. The crowd roared, thundering down heavy footsteps as they cheered.

The blood bar extended for miles, circling the perimeter of purgatory as souls lined up and got their drinks, ready to settle in for the fight they'd all been waiting for.

The crowd bellowed in excitement, savage and primal as Satan—*Lockie's* best demon—stepped into the ring. His nine-foot frame towered over Clyde who lounged, slack, up against the walls of the pit. He looked bored, but he felt anything but. I knew that, just as well as I knew myself.

Electricity ran through his veins as he waited to put on a show—a once-in-a-undead-lifetime—kind of show.

"Wooo!" I screamed. "That's my sugar, you kick his ass, baby!"

"Like he stands a chance. Ronagorg is Lockie's best demon!" Rory uttered in outrage as he turned eyes of fury onto me. The crowd closed in around me, the crowd that had dedicated themselves as our entourage.

Down here, we were kind of a big deal.

The underling King and Queen of the damned souls if you will.

I huffed, not at all intimidated by the hostility that approached me, from this low level demon and also Ronagorg's *horn buddy*. "You clearly don't know my baby. Clyde will wipe the floors of Hell with Ronagorg's face, then cheers us all to a round of his blood. Don't worry though, as his lover, I'm sure Clyde will give you the first shot." Indifferently I turned, taking away all of my attention with me. That infuriated the asshole who charged me with a clenched fist, not at all prepared for me to pull out a cut-down, semi-auto Remington Model 11 shotgun and blew a hole through his chest, sending his body skittering back to the ringside, where Clyde smirked at me with a vicious, predatory kind of smile.

Arousal pooled in my core and I shuddered, excited to see this fight through to the end so I could take my man home and show him exactly what he meant to me.

"Hey, Bon?" Tyler asked as he approached where I danced without care, not at all affected by what just happened.

The men and demons that swore their allegiance to me and Clyde, tighten their circle around me, even from the prince of Hell, all until I waved them off and reached for my whisky. "Let him through," I demanded. "Yes?"

"I know you just got back, but I was wondering, has anyone hired you for next All Hallows'?" he asked as he slunk himself into the seat beside me, elbows on the bar as he scanned the rowdy crowd who worshiped Clyde, but nowhere near as much as I did.

Down here, we had subsectors.

Different neighborhoods if you like.

Humans in one half of Hell, demons and other magical creatures in the other. And every single night, our worlds would cross as fights took place in the communal area we called the pit. It was the hot-spot hangout. Booze, women, men, and a fuck ton of entertainment and a chasm of sweaty sex. Although, our worlds would cross more than you would think, especially if a demon plucked one of the souls of the auction they are privy to of the human souls that get reaped or straight out of Devil's County itself.

Tyler cracked his neck, an excited chill skated down his spine as anticipation lit within his blue eyes, it was almost contagious, but I was off duty for the year.

"You know how it is, the second we step one foot in the grave the hounds descend, we've had more than a few approach us." I mused as I took a hefty sip of whisky, my eyes trained on Clyde's who watched me like a man in starvation.

"Figured as much, but listen. I'll triple the highest bid of Hell's Fire and I'll throw in four of my best men for you and Clyde to carve up. They're screamers," he bargained and I turned assessing eyes on him as I thought about it.

"How quickly do they heal?" I asked.

Down here, everybody heals. Even that asshole I just blew away and Hell's fire? It was demon currency in strength. There is a reason we're so powerful and can be seen when we come back from the dead. Others, if not shot up on the stuff, could only show themselves for small periods of time.

"They differ, but they'd last long enough to suit your fancy."

"Quadruple the Hell's Fire, give me ten of your best men

and throw in an invitation to the castle for Lockie's birthday. Clyde's is not long after the Devil's and he's always wanted to party with the Devil."

He looked at me and frowned. "You know he's my brother right?"

"Right."

"So, that is an easy one," he added. "Plus, you get invited every year, I don't know why you have to even ask. You bring him the most souls he's ever had down here."

"Never expected it to be difficult," I chuckled as I stood to my feet. "But I do expect you to go beg Lockie to go all out and do a grand gesture with the invitation. I know it will piss you off to have to ask anything from him, so it's the cherry on my cake."

"You're an evil bitch, you know that? This year he's bringing out the Queen succubus, you sure you want your man around that?"

"So I heard. Do you really think even a powerful whore could make my man stray?"

He looked back at Clyde and broke into a deep laugh. "Yeah, no. He would take her head and give her heart to the nearest perve to fuck while he told you all about it. You two are die-hard. Literally, considering you *died* together."

I scoffed a small laugh and rolled my eyes. "How original. What could you possibly need us for anyway? You know what our gig is. Anyone on earth you wanted to be killed, you could do it with the snap of your fingers."

"Yeah, well this is a game you see. One between me and Lockie. We have pawns up there, humans possessed with our best demons living like they are normal and shit. Thing is, that's part of the game. Staying hidden from the one who hunts you. So I need the two of you to sniff 'em' out, take 'em' out, and then declare I had absolutely *everything* to do with it. That... would be death-mate. I would have kicked his ass for the millionth time."

"You two are nuts, you know that?"

"Isn't that half the fun, doll." He smirked and I grinned at him. "These demons, they fuck shit up. Despite living as humans and shit, they appear as the worst kind. So right up your justice street. The deplorable things they do will be perfect for the fucked-up sex games you two play."

"Those in glass houses, Tyler," I scorned in a singsong voice that had him grinning from ear to ear.

"Will *come* on the shards of glass that stab them when it shatters, I know, I know. I need to hurry up and break mine."

"You warped fucker." I laughed.

"Hey, heads up. Your man is about to kick some ass."

We both turned toward the pit, Ronagorg roared and Clyde blew out a cloudy breath from his cigarette. He was still looking at me, those dark eyes filled with love, lust, and desire. My heart fluttered and I smirked because as soon as Ronagorg charged him, Clyde punched through his chest, ripped out his heart, and blew a cloud of smoke in his face.

Never having looked away from me once.

He's ride or die.

He's fucking King.

If you looked through all of the murders, you'd have noticed this is just our life after, fucked up and twisted, deplorable love story.

The End

ABOUT THE AUTHOR

Emmaleigh Loader is a stay-at-home mum of three - her two boys and her brother-in-law - and a wife, who lives in the UK.

Her favorite things are storms, the sea, and anything witchy! She finds winter beautiful and enjoys the beauty of the sun. She loves anything dark and adores loving alphas and strong women. She's an avid reader, and despite living with disabilities, pushes herself to be someone who her family, husband and sons are proud of.

Follow my socials:

https://linktr.ee/EmmaleighLoader

Also by Emmaleigh Wynters

Fantasy/Paranormal

Standalone:

Don't Read Between The Line's

Death's Wish - TBA

Devoured By The Lines TBA

ALSO BY EMMALEIGH LOADER

KING'S WOLVES MC

SAVAGE

OUIJA

STRAIGHTJACKET

STITCH

TOOTHPICK - TBA

A FALL FOR DESIRE:

The Last Time You Break Me: A Fall For Desire

NOVELLAS:

Who I Crave To Be

Daddy's Calling - TBA

IMPERFECTLY BEAUTIFUL

RISING FROM THE ASHES

Emmaleigh also has a series of notebooks.

The Witches series.

The Fantasy series.

(All Can Be Found Under Emmaleigh Loader On Amazon)

Merchandise:

Open Book: The VillainsThat Feed Our Soul Quoted Notebook.

Knife And Blood: The Villains We Need Notebook.

Girl In The Mind Library: Don't Read Between The Lines Quoted Notebook.

Black Unicorn: Savage Quoted Notebook.

Skull And Butterfly: Ouija Quoted Notebook.

Skeleton Couple: Stitch Quoted Notebook.

All notebooks will be live March 2022 on amazon. Other products with the merchandise designs will be available soon as well.